Magical Molly

&

the Beginning of the End

by

Bolton Williams

MAPLE
PUBLISHERS

Magical Molly & the Beginning of the End

Author: Bolton Williams

Copyright © 2025 1ST (New Edition) Bolton Williams

The right of Bolton Williams to be identified as author of this work has been asserted by the author in accordance with section 77 and 78 of the Copyright, Designs and Patents Act 1988.

First Published in 2025

Key Illustrator: Sharon Hinds

ISBN 978-1-83538-670-5 (Paperback)
　　　978-1-83538-671-2 (E-Book)

Book Cover Design and Layout by:
　　　White Magic Studios
　　　www.whitemagicstudios.co.uk

Published by:
　　　Maple Publishers
　　　Fairbourne Drive, Atterbury,
　　　Milton Keynes,
　　　MK10 9RG, UK
　　　www.maplepublishers.com

Magical Molly series

Book 1 – Magical Molly & the missing treasure.

Book 2 – Magical Molly & the beginning of the end.

Book 3 – Magical Molly & the Phorceg Cup.

Book 4 – Magical Molly & the ultimate treasure.

Book 5 – Magical Molly & Paradise Island.

Book 6 – Magical Molly & the family's betrayal.

Book 7 – Magical Molly arrives in Northern Ireland.

Book 8 – Magical Molly & the three Irish Kings

Book 9 – Magical Molly & Blue stack mountains.

Book 10 – Magical Molly & a family twist.

Book 11 – Magical Molly & the Cardiffians.

Book 12 – Magical Molly & the reading of the wills.

Book 13 – Magical Molly & the final encounter.

Pebble Powers and meanings-communication tool

Slate Pebble – News of utmost importance

Coal Pebble – Reasonable or strange news

Feather bound Pebble – Urgent reply required.

Orange Pebble – Long distance or abroad

Green Pebble – Castle messages

Glowing red Pebble – Imminent danger

Crystal, in silk pouch Pebble – No reply required.

CONTENTS

Black Annis confession

Tudor sat at the table in a state of shock as he listened to his long-term lover and witch, the reputable Black Annis. She had decided to tell her long-term partner the truth and nothing but the truth. The reasons for her mood swings and why she needed some sort of closure, even though it wasn't Tudors' fault at all.

She knew Tudor was about to leave again and help the family to secure the treasure but somehow today she couldn't take anymore. Tudor needed to know everything; he needed to know the truth.

Black Annis had been rejected years ago by the two step sisters who were witches of the first order. She had sired a daughter, and they had taken her baby away one evening without her knowledge. She had been banished. Tudor had discovered her in Harlech castle, acting as a maid for the Knights who were resident there at the time.

Tudor had been given a porkaht by her and inside was a lock of blond hair, the only part of her baby she had as a memory. As she explained everything to Tudor, his anger rose at an unprecedented level as he promised her, he would avenge the culprit one way or another. The porkaht had been given to her on the birth of her baby.

As he was digesting the information Black Annis shared with him, Tudor tried to compose himself. He loved her but he wasn't sure if he could forgive her. He would have to think about it, while he was away. He couldn't get his head around the facts. How could she and ... he had to get back to his imminent departure, as he shrugged the information to the back of his head for the time being.

Molly was arriving and he had not been given the opportunity to help guide her with his amazing spell capacity as Ivor had taken the decision, she would stay with him. This had also fuelled his anger with his brother. This family were notorious for keeping secrets, but Tudor wanted revenge. He had never been able to sire an heir, this was incomprehensible, what Annis had disclosed to him. Could he forgive her or the wizard in question even?

Not only he had this disclosure to contend with, but how dare Ivor take control of training Molly? This was the last straw and together with Black Annis, they set upon a deep spell as Tudor gave her the red collar, before he left for Saundersfoot.

Tudor couldn't get his head round the information Annis had shared with him. He gave her a strong sleeping draft to settle her down. He would return once the treasure hunt was over, and they would work out how to set the past right in the future.

He would personally find her missing daughter and he would personally set about a few long-standing spells to assist and hope to sweeten the revenge he felt right now. He summoned the resident black cat and started on his quest of revenge.

Prologue

The Llewellyn family had split up in various directions to gain the treasures at a quicker pace. This had seemed a good plan at the time but currently in Ivor's cave in Saundersfoot the mood was different.

There were outstanding issues to complete the finding of the treasure, even though they only had the Coracle to recover. The Hugglett spoon was safely inside Geraintus' jacket along with Yo-Yo who had been assigned to look after it above anything else. Geraintus, the gentle green giant, had to take the whispering fig tree to Castell Coch once this battle was over.

It was established that the Golden Treasure chest, the actual one, was safely hidden in the cavern of Castell Coch. It was imperative to move out of the cave in Saundersfoot and relocate their headquarters to Tongwynlais, which was a stone's throw away from Cardiff. Perfect for their newly confirmed status.

The family had realised that they needed to improve their communication system over the kingdom, since they had lost Gertrude. They also needed to be ahead of the kingdom in general, which would enhance their status as the First Family of Wales. The first family were always ahead of everyone else in the kingdom and this reputation had to be protected at all costs. This was becoming harder to fulfil.

They presumed through their deductions of the last riddle and the Crogg's movements that the genuine coracle was hidden somewhere in Llawhaden Castle. The family had split up to get the job done as the Crogg army, the Beggly army, were hot at their heels.

Kentav Crogg was determined to source the Hugglett spoon as he knew that this was another key treasure, he required to register his findings. He needed this treasure to secure and become the First Family of Wales. Whether he was entitled to have this treasure had suddenly not become an issue. He was obsessed.

Garibaldi tried to concentrate as it was imperative to fix the animals who appeared lifeless at that moment as time was of the essence. They had been severely injured at the onslaught on the beach with the Beggly army and the Croggs earlier in the day.

He was worried about Ivor, who was at Llawhaden Castle visiting his estranged cousin, Thomas Beckett. But he had no back-up in place right at that moment.

Elijas watched on with Tudor as the Wizard Bedivere and Garibaldi did their magic. Ginger One stirred but was badly charred and his left paw was hanging off a paw nail. Wibbly Alf the great chocolate St. Bernard had taken a big hit too and appeared lifeless as Bedivere was pouring a strong-smelling potion into his wounds.

Molly appeared more dazed than dead; however, she yet hadn't come round. How were they going to manage without her expertise, Elijas had no idea. After being in her company all this time, he'd realised even though reluctantly that she certainly knew her stuff and it was their own Ivor Ap Llewellyn, head of the family that was holding them back.

He had an incline about Ivor's past, but he wasn't going to be the one to tell anyone. He didn't want to gossip as he'd found out through listening to others. He would keep that firmly to himself.

He would disclose to Bedivere, who he thought had tried to take the treasure chest from Tudor, but again he wasn't sure if he should tell tales. Bedivere would need more evidence. He kept quiet. He would report to the Knights as usual, this he had managed to date to action, without any of the family noticing, that he was relaying the goings on in the cave.

Tudor was becoming more frustrated by the hour. He knew deep down that he had some responsibilities around the imminent disasters that the family were facing. He knew Ivor had deep dark secrets and he was determined that his own demons wasn't going to affect the family conquering the treasure.

Molly so impressed him, that he suddenly felt ashamed of what he had instigated with Black Annis witch before volunteering to help. If he had known the extend of Molly's attributes before her arrival, then he wouldn't have agreed to such a magnitude of spell.

Tudor started to feel a bit light headed knowing the irrevocable act, he had instigated with his partner. No one of the family knew of his liaison with this witch and that was the way he wanted it.

If Ivor knew the extent of his relationship, there would be murders. If Ivor knew he knew her, there would be murders. There was going to be murders at any rate, when Garibaldi twigged that the porkhat and the red collar had a link to each other. He thought that maybe Gari had more past knowledge, but Gari as a man servant was obliged to keep all secrets, just that. He was a bit uncomfortable to find out that the very cat he had trained along with the witch, was related to Slobbers. He had to keep away once all this was over. He felt a bit queasy, knowing this as...

"Tudor, you're daydreaming, concentrate."

Tudor shrugged himself back to the current dilemma as Gari gave him that look.

"Right. Tudor, Elijas, help us get the three of them on the couch. We can only wait for them to come round. The wounds will soon heal, they're more superficial than they look," sighed Gari relieved as was Bedivere.

***

Kentav Crogg, head of the Carpentry business in St. Clears and through his determination to be the First Family of Wales had lost his brother Trent to Manorbier castle. Trent was going to marry Katrin Crogg, apparently. He was utterly furious with him, and

Ali his other brother for not showing support in his quest for being the First Family of Wales.

Kentav knew things and he was not going to stop now, as he had retreated to St. Clears to gather more Begglys and foot soldiers. He was immensely popular since he'd captured the Golden Coracle right under the noses of the Llewellyn family and he wanted to capitalise on his newfound popularity and leadership.

Very soon, he would be living in a castle, the one he wanted was Cardiff, the capital city, where he could rule and be the first ever Crogg in the whole history of the Crogg family, to rule the kingdom. He couldn't wait.

Chapter 1

Slobbers

Garibaldi had watched the whole beach attack on the hovel and was ready for them, as Geraintus had opened the passageways in the cave not to waste time. Yo-Yo had watched the hovel too and had screeched when he had witnessed the three feathers coach hovering over the sand dunes. It was evident that there were injuries or fatalities.

"Yo-Yo keep calm, otherwise the spoon will start reacting. The coach will go back to Llawhaden quickly; we must just hope that they're only injured. Geraintus, get ready to fetch the whispering fig tree and take Yo-Yo and the spoon. I'll deal with the injured and then we'll leave as planned. Go, both of you."

Yo-Yo tried to protest as Garibaldi slipped his important collar on his neck. Yo-Yo hadn't worn this black studded collar since it had acted funny at the inauguration of the whispering fig tree. It had nearly choked him, and he was surprised that Gari had decided that this was the right time to wear it again. Geraintus gathered him up with the cushion and stuffed them both inside his large shirt. They departed into the first passage; the second passageway started huffing as the coach had landed.

The miners lantern

Gari opened the entrance immediately the green puff of smoke allowed him to see, as Geraintus and Yo-Yo disappeared. The coach doors slid open, and Harry and the cart fell out. There were three seriously injured family members on board and the wizards acted quickly.

"Quick Gari, we need to get them to the fireplace. Molly's burnt and in a bad way, and Wibbly Alf and Ginger Two are not responding. Elijas get the potions from the larder. Tudor re-seal the passageways, once the coach leaves. We need to sort this immediately," commanded Bedivere, aghast that they couldn't feel Wibbly's pulse or Ginger Two's.

***

At the front entrance of Llawhaden Castle stood Slobbers, who was losing patience with Ivor, especially as he'd suddenly realised that the three feathers coach had flown away in the direction of Saundersfoot. He was slightly perturbed that their get-away vehicle had gone without them. He only hoped it would return. This could only mean there was something wrong at the cave and this exasperated him even more.

"Have you got the sleeping draught Slobbers?" asked Ivor for the seventh time.

"Yes, Ivor and I'll drug Beckett's wine, once I've found the coracle giving me enough time to drag it to the coach which is no longer here," said Slobbers not wishing to alarm Ivor.

"Why has it gone?" said Ivor sounding anxious.

"It's hiding in a better place Ivor. I'm sure it will respond when I need it. Let's worry about the task in hand and announce ourselves. Then we can get on with it."

Slobbers didn't wish for any more dialogue about the problem that they seemed to have. They pressed the large gong which was at the side of the castle wall and waited for a sentry to greet them.

***

Garibaldi worked deftly and kept making weird smelly potions in his kitchen as Bedivere and Tudor, worked on the two dogs and Millie helped by working on Ginger Two. He hadn't had a chance to investigate the miners' lantern in the hallway. Yo-Yo had tried to tell him something regarding it, but the gang had crash landed in the passageway and had distracted him. Garibaldi had put the message via Yo-Yo's paw to the back of his mind, as resuscitating and repairing three injured animals, was of paramount importance.

Ginger Two had a paw hanging off by a nail and appeared dead. Molly was burnt in patches all over her body. Wibbly Alf was unconscious and even Garibaldis' deadly smelling salts hadn't yet revived any of them.

Bedivere and Tudor worked on them, and Millie copied the spells and potion giving on Ginger Two.

Ginger One disappeared outside to check on things as there was nothing he could do, while the wizards were working their diminishing magic. Bedivere left

Elijas and Tudor to continue with the calming spells and potion rubbing as he went to check the hovel. Garibaldi was adding all sorts of ingredients in the next batch and the cave began to stink.

"Keep rubbing this into Molly's fur Elijas, she needs to wake up urgently as indeed the other two," said Garibaldi as the next batch was ready.

Bedivere returned and looked anxious at Tudor and then Garibaldi.

"The Croggs look as if they're heading towards Llawhaden castle, there are hundreds of them. Gari go and check. Give me Ivor's wand, we need to get these animals fit right now."

Tudor gave Bedivere that look that said it all. Elijas began to feel frightened and continued to rub the potion into Molly's fur.

"Can we call Hopkin Paulinus to help us?" Elijas asked innocently.

"No, we can't," said Tudor quite curtly surprising Elijas. *"Hopkin Paulinus is the only wizard whose spells hasn't been affected. We can't afford to summon him back from Castell Coch when he's in the middle of sorting out those Eagles and preparing the castle for us to use as our new headquarters."*

"I didn't realise," said Elijas quietly as Bedivere looked up from Molly's body and saw horror on Garibaldi's face.

"What is it Gari?"

"It's the Beggly army; you're right Bedivere they're headed towards Llawhaden castle. We need to leave right away and rescue Ivor. These animals need to wake up now, or we've another problem."

"Did you kill Kentav Crogg?" asked Gari suddenly thinking aloud.

"No, but before we were attacked, he received a few double lighted arrows in his hat, which made him furious. He then realised we'd attacked over half his bug dogs and ordered a retreat command straight away. Zupp, who we've killed, his antennae's spark clashed with a few arrows and landed in Molly's cart which is why it exploded," explained Millie.

"We need to leave soon, at least we can rationalise with Kentav but not his programmed bugs," said Garibaldi as he checked the three animals at the hearth.

"Whatever happens, they'll have to come with us, in this state. We can't leave them here, as we're moving out," said Garibaldi as he wished that Geraintus and Yo-Yo hadn't left, they would have been extra support.

***

The tall overpowering sentry arrived at the gatehouse entrance and nodded for both Slobbers and Ivor to enter the castle. Fat Cat was perched on the top turret which overlooked the entrance, slid to an upright position, and yawned. He had to entertain these two *"has beens"* for his master and he wondered what they were doing at the castle as he trundled down to greet them. Not impressed at all.

Thomas Beckett was in the great hall waiting for them and greeted Ivor with open arms.

"Ivor, Slobbers, it's been too long. I was so pleased to get your message. Come, come, and dine with me, we've lots to discuss."

Ivor taken aback by this warm welcome went scarlet and felt foolish for having any doubts about him.

The table was long and narrow as Thomas beckoned for Ivor to sit opposite him. The two cats acknowledged each other and positioned themselves under the table next to their masters.

"We're on our way to Pembroke Castle and I thought a slight detour to see you would be prudent. We needed to sort out our differences and put the world to right," said Ivor trying to sound casual. He grabbed the goblet of wine and sipped some; to prove to Thomas he was happy to relax and chat.

"I'm pleased Ivor, but haven't you come looking for the coracle?" asked Beckett bluntly.

"Why is it here?" asked Ivor who tried to look surprised as this had been easier than he'd envisaged.

"Oh yes, Kentav Crogg left it here the other day, but he was clever," said Beckett.

"How so?" said Ivor as both Fat Cat and Slobbers paid attention and neither moved.

"He hid one of the coracles in the west dungeon, but he locked it a different way to the usual locking system, and we can't get in," said Beckett.

"Does he know we're here then?" asked Ivor trying to sound casual as Slobbers' fur started to rise on his tail, in anticipation of the next answer.

"Oh yes. I sent them a pebble the minute you sent an army of men here looking for a fugitive during Owain's battles. You must think I'm stupid Ivor."

"You've changed sides Beckett why," asked Ivor who had decided to get this over with, they obviously didn't have much time."

"Kentav offered me Caernarvon Castle, once they've located the treasure which according to him, is theirs. I want to live in a bigger more prestigious castle, it's quite simple," said Beckett who began to get agitated as he had to explain himself.

"The treasure isn't theirs to keep, let alone steal from us Beckett. The Croggs don't have a candle on their crest or standard. This is foolish of you Thomas. I can offer you a safe castle away from warriors and magical animals that could ruin your future. However, if you're that easily tempted by a four-foot Crogg who has no authority in these lands, then so be it. We shall eat and be on our way," said Ivor who sounded as exasperated as he felt.

"Let's just agree to have our differences Ivor," said Thomas who had decided he would side with the winner, regardless how he felt. He was still upset with Ivor about training Molly, but that issue could wait until he met her himself.

Thomas Beckett had been on the shortlist as one of the Knights to train the imminent Molly as his cat had the same, in fact equal powers to Ivor's, Slobbers. Just because Ivor was already head of the family had given him the edge in gaining the approval of everyone to train the Magical Molly, which Thomas Beckett had deemed grossly unfair.

Slobbers, under the table sent a quick pebble to Garibaldi warning them that the Croggs were imminent. He thought fast and started to act out his plan knowing he had to get Fat Cat on his side.

"Let's look at the dungeon, the one you can't open. I'll try and open it for you, so that you'll look good for your master?" whispered Slobbers under the table.

"That would really be helpful," said Fat cat beginning to like this equally big cat.

They both slipped out of the great hall, while Ivor and Thomas had changed the subject and were discussing the battles round the region in earnest.

"It can't be fun here on your own," said Slobbers trying to be friendly.

"Why do you say that?" asked Fat cat leading Slobbers to the west dungeon door.

"Well, I've several magical animals in my house, a horse and we have lots of fun inventing new ideas and helping the wizards come up with new spells and stuff."

"Sounds great but Beckett is my master and even though I get frustrated with him at times, that's how it is," said Fat cat sighing a little.

They stood outside the dungeon and Slobbers tried the big round knob that looked like a door handle. He'd been given instructions and information from both Molly and Garibaldi and decided it was time to disclose it.

"Where's the lock?" asked Slobbers.

"You've got something to tell me, haven't you?" said Fat cat.

"How do you know?"

"You just screwed up your whiskers like you know something. I do the same, that why."

"Yes, sit down Fat, I've something to tell you, but we must hurry," said Slobbers thinking he might have to drug him once he'd told him this story.

"We're brothers, Fat. When we lived with that crook, we were too young to know anything. Our mother took us to different castles to keep us safe. She left you with Thomas Beckett as you were the important one and you could manage him by yourself. She gave Garibaldi instructions to inform you when a great decision had to be made. This decision is now upon us. I need my brother on my side and not the enemy. This place is going to be under attack very soon as the Croggs are on their way, what do you think?" said Slobbers.

Slobbers looked at this big puss and hoped the shock wasn't going to create more havoc.

"But how and when and why wasn't I given a name?" replied Fat cat quite shocked.

"You were given a grand name but the old crook who had us couldn't remember it, so Fat cat was easier," explained Slobbers examining the complicated looking lock on the door. He let the information sink in as it was going to be life changing for Fat Cat.

"What is it then?"

"It's Fabbles, how great is that?"

"Wow really, my name is Fabbles," beamed Fabbles.

"Yep, come on help me get this door open before the Croggs get here. Is there anything you can do? I haven't heard from Gari, I don't know how long we've got before they turn up," said Slobbers getting to work.

"I'll go and check on the sentry points, while you open the door. We mustn't tell Beckett any of this, unless he makes friends with Ivor," said Fabbles and disappeared as quickly as a fat cat could.

Slobbers who'd been brought up by that crook as part of a litter of kittens, had at least taught him well as he realised this as he was picking the lock. He'd taught him to carry a set of special tools in his pouch and how to use each claw on his clever paw. He was able to ascertain how long a claw he needed by the thickness of the door.

He thought of Fabbles and wondered what had happened to the other three brothers as they'd been a litter of five boys. At least he'd found one brother, which was something. There had also been a pure white pup amongst them which had been brought up with them partially at least. The pup had been constantly with the fairies, Slobbers shrugged. He'd forgotten about that until now. He tried to rack his brains to remember the names of the other three cats. He'd have to think about that once this was over. He had to concentrate. How bazaar that this had come to his mind right now.

Once they'd finished treasure hunting, he would try and find the others. The lock was taking longer than he'd hoped. He knew that Thomas Beckett was a traitor and there was no way, he was going to allow Fabbles to stay at this castle with him.

Chapter 2

Llawhaden Castle

Tudor was outside the cave, and he was preparing the three feathers coach to take them all to Llawhaden castle. Thankfully, Garibaldi and Bedivere had revived everyone, but they were weak. This was not what they'd expected as they were now three short to rescue Ivor and Slobbers.

Time was of paramount importance. They decided to bring Harry and the cart, in order that Wibbly, Ginger Two and Molly could continue to rest on the journey. They desperately needed Molly functional as their spells were dwindling but they had to make the best of the situation. Tudor had returned and changed into a battle cloak which comprised of a deep red mooned ensemble. He looked a bit like a raging bull with his fiery red cloak shiny and new. It was also sporting red candles which alighted if you got a bit too close as Garibaldi's beard had discovered as he'd passed him a moment earlier.

Garibaldi had shocked everyone by sporting a turquoise cloak with candles and little half-moons. He had changed everyone's collars especially Molly's as she laid conscious but nowhere well enough for a battle with Croggs and bug dogs. He was worried.

"Elijas secure the passageways' and bring the lantern with us. Bedivere, can you bring the hovel, we need to take everything we've already packed. It's time everyone let's go, Ivor and Slobbers need our help. We'll discuss on the way, how we're going to attack the Croggs and help Ivor and Slobbers at the same time. Plus, if we've been right, we've a coracle to rescue," said Garibaldi knowing he needed more than a few magical spells. He was praying for a miracle of mammoth proportions.

Elijas stood in the hallway and noticed a parchment under the lantern as he went to collect it for travelling.

"Look Gari, there's something under the lantern, shall I bring it?"

"Oh yes, Yo-Yo told me earlier. It's important Elijas keep it safe until I need it," said Garibaldi as he realised what Yo-Yo had done and had momentarily forgotten. He tutted to himself and hoped he wasn't beginning to lose his marbles, like the wizards. He busied himself knowing they were ready to leave.

Crash.......... Crash!!

Whatever was that?

Geraintus fell out of the secret passageway that Tudor and Bedivere had spent the last hour sealing. He spluttered dust all over Tudor who stood there displeased. Bedivere had to wave his hand and murmur some spell to disperse the cloud. Tudor was still spluttering as Gari said,

"*Why are you not protecting Yo-Yo, Geraintus? He has the spoon; your orders were not to leave them out of your sight?*" said Gari quite frustrated with everything that was occurring.

"*He's disappeared. We were in the tree hiding. I fell asleep and when I woke up, he was gone. I've searched everywhere and everything, he's gone, and the spoon has gone too. I've searched my house, grounds, everywhere and thought best to come straight away to tell you before you left,*" said Geraintus in obvious distress. "*He knew to stay inside my tunic, but I've turned it inside out and he's gone.*"

"*Have you asked the tree?*" asked Tudor who knew they were now indeed in trouble.

"*Yes, I've done everything, all the whispering tree says, is check the lantern. But there's no lantern at my quarters, that's why I came here.*"

"*Elijas, give me that parchment you found,*" said Gari as the penny dropped slightly but he wasn't quite sure. "*We found a parchment under our lantern earlier Geraintus. I presume this will tell us where Yo-Yo has hidden the spoon. We'll read it in the coach. Geraintus, you must uproot and take the tree to Castell Coch. We're leaving in a few minutes once we secure that passageway again. I'm sure Yo-Yo is safe, we must get to Ivor before the Croggs get there,*" said Garibaldi as he waved his hand as a signal for everyone to move out. He read the parchment, but it didn't make sense. He stuffed it in his pocket until they got on the coach.

Ivor's Saundersfoot secluded cave

"How do you know Yo-Yo is safe?" asked Tudor feeling quite confused suddenly.

"He wasn't happy to be left out of this imminent battle with the Croggs, even the one on the beach. He's got a plan to help us somewhere along the way I'm sure," said Bedivere trusting what instincts he had remaining.

"Right, let's go," ordered Garibaldi his stomach churning in knots knowing Slobbers may need help with Ivor. They were three animals down and now they weren't sure if the spoon was hidden with Yo-Yo. Ginger Two was left inside the cave, safe but too unwell to travel. He needed to totally recover in a quiet space and the family would come back for him.

"Everyone, in the cart."

The wizards climbed in next to Molly and Wibbly and the rest of the animals followed. Gari threw some angel dust in the air and spelled the cave which disappeared temporarily to Narberth, but more importantly it was no longer on view on the beach.

"Baja Solana/ Bahia Solanah," he repeated three times as he threw more fairy dust in the air and the Three Feathers coach, with new reinforced glass windows and doors, hovered over towards them.

"Trynhedfan Piwssagwyrdd / Treenheadvan peewsagweerth," he again repeated three times as the cart, with all the family aboard raised in the air and darted very swiftly inside. The coach swirled speedily under Gari's continued spell and quickly disappeared towards Llawhaden Castle.

A groan and a grunt came from the centre of the cart as Millie excitedly shouted,

"Wibbly's waking up."

Bedivere looked at Tudor and then Gari as all three were quietly urging Molly to fully wake up.

"Let me read Yo-Yo's message. We'll be at Llawhaden in no time, and we need to sort this out along with a plan of attack once we get there," said Garibaldi trying to ignore how he and the wizards were really feeling.

"The wind is very windy; the sand is very sandy. The tree is white or is it green? It's safe to look and to be seen. The lightning will and will not strike. I will fight and put this family right."

"This isn't too bad to understand," said Elijas feeling a bit more confident as he'd found the parchment in the first place.

"What do you think?" said Garibaldi who had some idea but wasn't sure.

"The lightning's are the Begglys, surely?" said Elijas.

"Yes, and the whispering fig tree is green," said Tudor. *"Okay, the rest is obvious. We're going into battle so what's the clue?"* asked Tudor who realised for the first time how difficult these riddles were. Ivor had to cope with situations like these on a regular basis, it was no wonder he always looked as if he was losing the plot.

"I know the answer. Let's rescue the coracle with Ivor and Slobbers, right away," responded Molly as she

woke up and sat upright to everyone's relief, especially Garibaldi.

Millie checked Molly's fur as Bedivere gave her the turquoise collar to wear.

"Gari, send Slobbers a pebble to open the back gate," as Wibbly's tail, weak but functional swished open the top of the three feathers coach operating system, exposing the feathers as they knitted together gathering local data.

The coach hovered in the field near to the castle as they waited for the pebble to return.

***

Slobbers was nearly there; he could feel the latch and the bar on the inside begin to loosen as he wriggled with his longest claw inside the lock. He wondered how Fabbles felt after he'd been told he'd four brothers and he'd just found one. He was a long time, he hoped that Ivor was still entertaining Thomas, and no one had missed them.

Seeing Fabbles react and knowing he had other brothers out there had brought a few surprise memories of his kittenhood. He decided he would share with Molly as she needed to know there was a fourth brother. He hadn't remembered until now, but Molly hadn't mentioned him when she was sharing the task he had to perform with the Coracle. He'd tell her once all of this was over. He must tell her about the white pup that had been brought up with them too.

As his thoughts gathered momentum so was his claw and eventually, he heard a sigh and a clanking sound and the round, knocker type handle on the front door turned; it was unlocked.

At this moment, Fabbles came running out of breath and stopped in astonishment to see the door open.

"Slobb, bruv, there's a glass coach hovering in the back garden and this plopped by my feet. It's for you, I think. We must get back as Ivor and Thomas are both drunk and are beginning to argue."

Slobbers quickly read the pebble, and he was pleased at how Fabbles was reacting to his news.

"We've three things to do Fabbles."

"Tell me."

"You must go and open the back gate at once and let the coach in. Get back to under the table with Thomas and Ivor and I'll get some mead with the sleeping draught in it. We'll both wait under the table until Beckett's asleep. We mustn't look too friendly with each other."

"Yes of course, what's the third thing?"

"You're coming home with us," said Slobbers hugging his brother for the very first time.

Fabbles ran off and opened the back gate to the castle. The guard was due back in twenty minutes from the village. He'd have to think of something to distract him, if his new family were still in the castle retrieving the coracle.

***

"The Croggs are a mile away and there's about a hundred and fifty bug dogs, enough to give us trouble," said Garibaldi as he deciphered the three feathers coded messages which poured out of the dash like peppered paper.

"The back-gate's opening," said Elijas who was on look out near the top deck windows.

"Right," said Molly, who hadn't planned anything with anyone up until that point.

"Harry and gang, you'll trot in as if you've a cargo of coal to deliver to the castle just in case you get stopped. Once inside make your way to the dungeon area and find Slobbers. He should have opened one of the doors by now, but wait for me, in case he hasn't managed to get it done."

"Newid, Newid ar unwaith/ Nehweed Nehweed arh eenwah-eeth," as she repeated it three times swishing her tail scattering more angel dust over Harry and everyone in the coach.

As in Yo-Yo's poem, it could be seen, but it wouldn't look like it was, but no one had worked this out yet.

"The rest of us will follow in a minute. We've got our spells," said Molly as the animals looked on aghast to be going in without her. *"You'll be hidden and look like coal as soon as you jump into Harry's cart. Be ready for Croggs and use your new spells. Ginger One, be lookout once the dogs are inside with the coracle,"* instructed Molly.

Millie and Wibbly Alf jumped into the cart, as they knew and realised that their link chain and collar would calm the coracle on sight. Slobbers would need help to move it. Harry brayed, swishing his magically dusted tail and the coach opened its doors as they careered down the steps and went towards the main gates of the castle.

Geraintus, who had marched towards Llawhaden, after he had delivered the whispering fig tree to Castell Coch; had arrived at the gate just in time. The wizards summoned him to join them and listen to the plan to retrieve the coracle.

"Good timing Geraintus, did you see the Croggs?" asked Bedivere anxious his friend could have been ambushed on his way.

"Yes, they're about an hour away, we must hurry."

"Right Tudor, come with me," said Molly. *"We'll walk in to find Thomas. If we get stopped, we're just visiting. Bedivere, Elijas and Geraintus patrol the perimeter and watch out for the guards, who should be back from the village at any moment. Kill them if necessary but keep them away from the castle."*

Geraintus looked at Bedivere who could see that they needed their spells to work at this moment. To avoid the Croggs was no longer an option. Elijas went pale but realised he had to either step up or no longer be a seemingly part of the Llewellyn family.

"What about Kentav Crogg?" asked Bedivere.

"Keep him talking and pretend we're here on a social call and if he asks, you've no idea where the coracle is hidden, and quiz him about it. He won't kill us, not yet at least. Until he has all the treasure in his grasp. Remember he's looking for the spoon," reminded Molly. *"Bedivere, keep the coach floating behind this tree and keep it running. We'll leave together with the coracle. We must go Tudor."*

Tudor and Molly left quickly and made their way into the castle unnoticed through the back open entrance. They made their way to the great hall, where they could hear shouting and bad language coming from the dining area. They hid behind the thick velvet curtain and observed Ivor and Thomas Beckett arguing about their cats and shouting at each other.

Slobbers swished his tail towards Molly, and she knew the sign. Any moment now, the sleeping draught in Thomas's goblet would take effect. They had to wait.

Within minutes Thomas's head fell into his pudding as the powerful potion took hold. Immediately, Tudor and Molly ran out to Ivor who looked very relieved to see them.

"Thank goodness. I didn't realise how long it was going to take. He's terribly upset with me and all the family," said Ivor.

"He'll be even more upset when he wakes up with a headache which will last until Christmas Ivor. We need to move him to the kitchen and tie him up, even though

he'll be asleep for a while," said Tudor who began to drag him over to the kitchen area with Ivor assisting.

"Ivor meet us at the dungeon, I'll go with Fabbles and Slobbers right away to get the coracle out," said Molly. *"We haven't much time."*

"Follow me," said Fabbles pleased to be a part of this family.

The three ran towards the dungeon leaving Tudor and Ivor to secure Thomas Beckett, to be sure.

The animals were waiting by the open door as Harry the horse was grazing outside the perimeter waiting to collect the coracle. Wibbly Alf with a nod from Molly went ahead, down the steep narrow steps of the dungeon immediately followed by Millie, Ginger One, Tudor and Molly. Slobbers and Fabbles followed them, leaving the dungeon door ajar.

The Golden Coracle was tied to three poles and looked suffocated and sad. The moment the family entered the room; it began to show its golden colour brightening up the dingy dungeon with some light. A fat rat scurried away from the area as the family ran down the stone steps.

"Slobbers, do you want to jump in and see if you can get your paw underneath and unlock it?" asked Molly, which surprised everyone. It was automatically thought that as Molly was the most magical; she would be the one who was going to administer the spells of the Golden Coracle.

Golden coracle in the dungeon

"Yes okay," said Slobbers feeling immensely proud in front of his newly found brother.

***

"I wish they'd hurry up, the Croggs are in our sight," said Bedivere as he'd just deciphered the messages coming from the Three feathers' dashboard.

"They haven't been that long Bedivere, patience. I'm as anxious as you are," said Garibaldi wanting to see Ivor safe which was natural as his master.

"I'm going to kill Kentav Crogg the minute I set eyes on him; I'm fed up with the whole family fiasco he's created for us."

"I'll do it for you Gari," whispered Geraintus. *"I've less conscience than you, leave him to me."*

"Elijas move the coach inside the castle grounds, leave it hovering by that tree, it's time we went inside to help. The Croggs will spot us here if we don't hurry."

***

Elijas was the first to hit the ground with a thud as the antennae of the bug dog caught him square on the back of the neck. He didn't have a chance to retaliate with a spell. Geraintus started to huff and puff as a few antennae caught his legs. However, Garibaldi was safely inside the castle walls as was Bedivere. Geraintus jumped over the wall and tried to avoid the flying sparks. He started to repair his wounds by giant magic potions. Suddenly they seemed surrounded as

38

they saw Kentav's tall Welsh hat appear and then his round face, redder than normal.

"Who else is with you," he demanded as his shrill echoed around the inner curtain.

"It's just us, visiting Thomas Beckett," retorted Bedivere, who wished Geraintus would just finish him off, there and then. Suddenly Bedivere realised as did Garibaldi, that Kentav had no idea how many family members were at the castle.

"Why are you using the back entrance?"

"Our coach dropped us here by mistake," said Garibaldi trying not to sound fearful as he shuffled for the red pebbles in his pocket.

"I'll call Thomas Beckett for you. Don't move a muscle, bug dogs move in," ordered Kentav giving three bug dogs instructions to kill them if they moved position.

"No problem," whispered Garibaldi as they all watched with horror as Elijas' dead body was being dragged away from the entrance.

Gari moved closer to Bedivere as Geraintus stood behind as he towered over them. He'd finished repairing himself and then he whispered to them,

"There must be a hundred bug dogs surrounding the castle outside."

"We daren't move those three bug dogs on the wall have perfect aim, they've just killed Elijas, what do we do know?" asked Bedivere as he watched Garibaldi

fumbling in his pocket. He stood close to Bedivere and showed him three red pebbles. Bedivere gave him a knowing nod as Gari threw them in the air.

The three red pebbles went plop, never to be seen again as the antennae of the bug dogs were fully focused on them and ready to kill them if they moved a muscle.

Chapter 3

The Golden Coracle

Plonk! Plonk! Plonk!!

"What's that?" asked Tudor as they all watched Slobbers trying to get his paw underneath the chains to access the seat.

"A pebble. Oh, my goodness, there's three. Fabbles quick go outside and get me a status report and check on Beckett. Something's happened," said Molly. *"Ivor, move Harry somewhere more secure, for when we need him."*

Ivor decided to go immediately without the need to clarify the red pebble problem; he felt he'd done his bit.

"Wibbly, Millie use your collars and try to unfasten the chains from the poles. Tudor start on your chanting spells, the ones you know, for when it needs to start its own spell giving. It looks distressed; we need to liven it up as otherwise it's not going to marry up with the spoon."

It was quite dark in the dungeon with only slits of light coming through the gaps in the stonework. The odd rat scurried past as the family concentrated on the task in hand. Tudor started murmuring the enchanted spells as Slobbers sat, stuck, on top of the ash seat with his paw firmly secured underneath.

41

Molly jumped on the seat to help him, and the little crests and moons started to dance as if to recognise Molly's paws. This encouraged Molly to unleash Slobbers quickly.

"They're coming loose," shouted Wibbly as the poles wriggled and fell to the floor. Immediately all the chains unravelled, and the golden coracle was set free.

"Wibbly, Millie, Ginger, over here," instructed Molly. *"Join tails quickly and copy me."*

She took Slobbers' paw and together they unravelled a box under the seat as Slobbers could feel her strength.

"Kayealexaly, Kayealexaly; free yourself to us, your Llewellyn family. Huggle-Puggle, Huggle-Puggle, we're not trouble. Whispering fig tree is green and not white. Golden Coracle mustn't have a fright. Wake up to Kayealexaly, Kayealexaly now."

Molly stood on the seat raising her tail in the air as the others copied and watched as the Golden Coracle turned the room pink, then purple and eventually the whole room became a warm turquoise, which matched their collars.

"No one move," Molly commanded as Tudor was about to take a step forward as he watched this moment of magic. He realised that Molly was indeed more magical than he'd given her credit and would endeavour to make amends when all this was over. He would even confess and apologise to Ivor once all this fiasco was done with.

The Golden Coracle spun round slowly for everyone to admire it. The little half-moons on the seat were dancing around Molly's feet. The golden link chain, with the two missing links was upright and looking for its links. The coracle danced with apparent relief and happiness. They all knew that it was only a matter of time, that they would link the spoon to complete the magical strength of the family.

"Introduce yourselves to the coracle, in turn. It will protect us on our journey to Castell Coch," instructed Molly.

Wibbly was nearest and he placed his link chain towards the coracles' chain. It joined together like a magnet which confirmed, not that it was necessary that Wibbly was a family member and had found the right chain. Millie went towards the coracle next and held its chain in her most magical paw. Immediately the coracle spun round, and the room went purple. Everyone barked as Millie's tail wagged a thousand times, she'd always been a Llewellyn.

Fabbles came pounding down the steps and disrupted the coracles' flow, as Tudor stopped him for a second. He had grave news, but it had to wait for a minute. He stood on the steps of the dungeon and watched Slobbers being introduced to the coracle properly for the first time. Slobbers placed his paw under the seat and found the box. He looked at Molly, who nodded.

The box opened and five lockets fell out, one had S inscribed on it. Slobbers took the locket, and it fitted the eyelet hole of the Golden Coracles' chain, and the coracle spun from side to side and confirmed and acknowledged Slobbers as family.

He was a Llewellyn. The coracle was dancing as everyone turned to Fabbles who was flabbergasted to find his brother was a Llewellyn. What did that make him?

"Yes, you're a Llewellyn too and Ginger One is also your brother. These are your lockets, but we've problems to attend. We'll celebrate your news later. Fabbles, give us a status report," said Molly who'd guessed they had trouble ahead.

"Garibaldi, Geraintus and Bedivere are being held and surrounded by thirty bug dogs, and there's about a hundred bug dogs surrounding the castle. Elijas is dead. Kentav Crogg is trying to wake up three sentries, but I've drugged them. He hasn't discovered Beckett yet, but he is still asleep."

"Is there only one Crogg?"

"Yes."

"Slobbers, Fabbles, go and attack Kentav Crogg and tie him up with the sentries, bring his Welsh hat back with you for Ginger One."

The two big cats disappeared, and the others stood waiting for instructions.

"Ginger, once they get back with the hat, you must go and impersonate Kentav over the wall. The bug dogs will only see the hat. Let's hope they believe you when you order them to retreat. It's worth a try. We need Gari, Geraintus and Bedivere down here to help us get the coracle up the steps," said Molly. *"Go straight away."*

Ginger was pleased to have his abilities recognised by Molly especially as he'd discovered he had two new brothers; he was ecstatic and even more determined to do a decent job.

"Can we not leave here in invisible mode?" asked Millie.

"No," said Tudor and Ivor together.

Tudor was feeling rather guilty and remorseful and couldn't tell anyone. Not only had he trained a deadly cat. He had trained the cat to administer an unbreakable spell. The cat had brothers,' and they were right here, and not just Slobbers, he quietly felt sick.

Molly looked at Millie who looked desperate and knew how she felt. She was beginning to lose the ability to think of a way out of this mess too. She was still suffering from the last attack and had to concentrate fully and think clearly as they were all relying on her.

"Once the coach is in our sights, we can be invisible, Millie. But there's a castle fortress between us right now, and it wouldn't work. Remember, our spells even mine are diminishing, until we get the treasures together. We can only hope the cats will be back in a moment having tied up Kentav. Tudor, there must be another way out of

here. Wibbly, Millie, go and investigate further down the dungeon and see what you can find."

***

Slobbers and Fabbles didn't need to be told twice. They scurried quickly towards the castle perimeter to observe Kentav. Kentav was handing out instructions to the Begglys, his little arms were flying up and down in all directions as he organised the bug dogs round the castle. They were hiding behind the gate pillar, and they could see that there were three Begglys positioned on the wall in front of a tired and scared looking Bedivere, Geraintus and Garibaldi.

Slobbers felt a wave of anger as he saw how much his master was struggling to keep his composure as they were trapped. There were thirty Begglys around them also and he nodded at Fabbles as he spotted a way of attacking Kentav without being attacked by the Begglys.

He couldn't wait to get his claws in Kentav for the last time.

***

Ivor, who was sat and positioned on the steps after he had re-routed Harry and the cart as someone needed to be on look out. The dungeon door swung open suddenly and Garibaldi ran down the steps nearly knocking Ivor sideways. Bedivere and Geraintus were close behind him. Garibaldi was as white as a sheet as he relayed Elijas' death, to reiterate the pickle they were in.

"We're surrounded Molly," said Bedivere. *"The cats have nearly killed Kentav, he's out of it for the moment and they've tied him up. The bug dogs have re-grouped, but they've surrounded the castle as they're not sure what to do next."*

Molly knew that they all wondered why she wasn't at the front of this attack. She recognised at that moment that her spells were weak as she wasn't fully recovered. She needed to show strategy skills right away, for the family to regain their faith in her. She knew that Slobbers understood the reason she'd sent him and Fabbles to ambush Kentav. They were stronger than her at this moment.

BARK! BARK! BARK!

As Wibbly barked with excitement, Millie was carrying something in her mouth. The dungeon door opened in a hurry and a proud Slobbers and Fabbles ran down the steps.

"Slobbers, Fabbles well done, is he secure?"

"For the time being," nodded Slobbers who was covered in more blood than his brother.

"Ginger go with the hat and try and send the bug dogs to retreat. Wibbly, Millie what have you found?"

Molly suddenly was in full command. Ginger waited to see what the dogs had found before he left as he sat on the top step watching.

"Goodness," said Ivor as he investigated as Tudor also quickly realised what they'd discovered.

"They're lighted arrows, similar to the ones we used yesterday at the beach," said Ivor astonished.

"How many are there?" asked Molly thinking fast.

"We can treble the amount right away," said Bedivere waving his hand in the air as more bundles appeared and scattered as they toppled over each other.

"We need to fight the bug dogs and try and disperse them, even though Ginger is going to have a go in a moment. They don't know you're here Molly; we'll keep it that way. Gari, Geraintus and I will take these and throw them over the wall. We'll try and get rid of as many bugs before you come out with the coracle," suggested Bedivere.

"Tudor set them all up to alight once they're ready to be thrown," instructed Molly not liking this idea one bit as she noticed Garibaldi shuddering at the very thought. There was no choice; they all had to get back to the coach separately or together. Soon the bug dogs would be inside the Castle and in the dungeons looking for them. That would be disaster for them all. At least being in the chapel quarters, they had a slim few minute's thinking time.

"This is what we're going to do everyone. Gari, Geraintus and Bedivere will go. Fabbles, Slobbers and Ginger can carry the bundles out as they won't necessarily look at you three as the enemy. Geraintus, go first as you tower over everyone and can shield them for a bit. If you make your way up to the five-storey tower porch to attack, Fabbles you know the way. You'll get a

clear view below, and you all have good aim. Once you've got a clear view of the coach, behind the oak tree and its safe you must all head towards it. No one is going to wait for anyone, is that clear. You must all get to the coach before I bring the coracle. Tudor go with them. Your arrow throwing is highly accurate and the more Llewellyn's Kentav sees when he gets loose from his ties, the less likely he'll think that Ivor and I are missing. The three of us with Ivor will manage the coracle."

"You need support here, Molly."

"No Tudor, you must get to the coach, we're not waiting for anyone once this coracle gets rescued. It's best you go ahead," insisted Molly.

The three cats disappeared with bundles on their shoulders followed by a distraught Gari, but Geraintus and Bedivere placed him in the middle, and they left. Tudor followed equally determined and suddenly overcome with dreadful guilt, but he didn't want to be left behind.

Ivor got to work on the coracle with the dogs with Molly's instructions and lifted the coracle up the dungeon steps to leave.

"The door won't open," said Ivor trying with all his strength to turn the large round handle.

"The guys have just left Ivor. Let me try," said Molly as she placed the coracle down on the step with Wibbly holding the weight from toppling over and went to the door.

Molly knew, as fear passed over her along with the need to find another solution to this ever-increasing mess, they were in.

"Bring the coracle back down," said Molly as Millie and Wibbly helped Ivor to place it back in its original position.

Ivor tried to open the door but to no avail. Molly was quickly back on the top step, she tried again and confirmed what she knew.

"The doors' been locked twice from the other side. Kentav must have been untied by the sentries, he's obviously going to take the coracle from us."

"There's no time to waste, Wibbly, Millie. We need to look further down the dungeon and see if there's another way out of here. Thomas Beckett built this fine castle; he is re-known for clever constructions. Don't tell me that he hasn't built a secret door in every dungeon and hideaway in this castle. There must be something we've missed. Surely, he'd have made provisions for an escape access somewhere, Ivor?"

The three dogs went searching as Ivor looked exasperated and helpless. He knew that he should know more about his so-called family. He was becoming more uneasy by the hour.

***

Geraintus had followed Fabbles, who led the way, and the party got up to the fifth storey without much attention.

"Start throwing guys. We need to get rid of these bug dogs and if you see Kentav, he's mine," ordered Geraintus not forgetting what he and Garibaldi had discussed prior to this mess.

The bug dogs on the ground surrounded the castle wall and were initially taken by surprise as the Llewellyn party could observe where the hot spots were on the ground.

Geraintus was throwing arrows with such force and accuracy that Bedivere was just handing him the arrows. Garibaldi was giving Tudor arrows, he was as accurate as Geraintus as the arrows lit up in flames as they flew, hitting the targets.

"Look, there's Kentav, quick Geraintus, do it," shouted Garibaldi as he handed him a big fat arrow.

"Retreat, retreat," commanded Kentav as a large bug dog threw himself at the castle wall, which sent a large spark towards the Llewellyn's hitting Bedivere in the shoulder as he fell to the ground.

"He's all right, don't stop. Doesn't Kentav look odd without his tall hat," shouted Tudor aiming at Kentav as Geraintus missed but Bedivere got hit again.

"Retreat," shouted Kentav again as an arrow caught his orange tuft of hair as he looked up and saw the wizards throwing lighted arrows and he went berserk. He was covered in blood and deep scratches where Slobbers and Fabbles had sprung him earlier. He was furious.

How dare someone steal his Crogg Topper, his Welsh hat, and did they think he was that stupid? He'd found Thomas Beckett drugged 'till Christmas and he'd guessed the Llewellyn's were in the dungeon. That's why he'd locked it. No one could get in as the fool Beckett had told him how to double lock it.

He would leave and let those stupid idiots think they'd won and return with more bugs at first light. They'd never be able to open that door, and he would take the coracle back to St. Clears. At least in his shop there were plenty of people who could keep an eye on it.

He couldn't see Molly and guessed that she was in the dungeon securing the coracle. Well, she would have to prove how truly magical she really was as the lock was spelled tight. He smiled through gritted teeth as another arrow grazed his forehead singeing his orange tuft of hair.

"Retreat," he hollered once more, and the remaining bug dogs turned towards him, and moved quickly following Kentav away from the castle.

"Quick, they're retreating. We need to get Bedivere out of here," shouted Tudor.

"We need to get back to the dungeon. I can repair him better there," said Garibaldi, *"We can all leave the dungeon together; we must hurry as he'll be back with more of those bug dogs before nightfall."*

Fabbles and Slobbers had run ahead and had found the dungeon door locked. It took a few extra minutes for

Slobbers to unhinge the lock again, but once it opened, he swished his tail over it.

"What are you doing?" asked Fabbles.

"Kentav double locked it from this side. Once the wizards get here, I've put a spell on it, which makes it look like it's locked but we can still open it from the inside."

"Cool."

Ginger One appeared suddenly in front of the wizards who were not as fast as they should be.

"Where did you get to?" asked Slobbers.

"Been checking the perimeter and talking to the sentries. The bug dogs are near to here, they're Kentav's back up. He'll be back very soon. We need to get the coracle out immediately. They've just moved Elijas's body from the entrance. We can't get to him even if we wanted to."

The three cats let the wizards down the steps into the dungeon. Geraintus carried Bedivere as Tudor was murmuring spells and Garibaldi had already started on his wounds. Blood was dripping throughout the passage, but no one took much notice.

⊷⊷⊷◅▷⊷⊷⊷

Chapter 4

The legend of Yo-Yo

Yo-Yo held on tight. Hiding in Geraintus' green baggy tunic inside the secret pocket lining was no picnic. He'd had to stifle a laugh when Geraintus had got all hot and bothered whilst looking for him. He knew he would understand. He'd administered one of his learnt spells from Molly. Geraintus wouldn't have been able to feel his presence under his shirt. He was there all of this time.

The thing was, he'd arrived with Molly to save her, and the family and the time had come. He'd also disobeyed orders by leaving the Hugglett spoon spelled and secure but safely hidden. Molly had understood his poem; he was satisfied all his work was done.

He was delighted that the cats had discovered they were brothers, a secret Molly had shared with him on their way from Spain. That seemed a long time ago since they had had that conversation. He also hoped that Molly was eventually ready to tell everyone what was bothering her as she'd a treasure of her own to find.

He snuggled further down Geraintus' tunic as things were going to get tricky.

"*How's Bedivere?*" said Molly as she summoned all three cats, to prepare them to leave.

"*He'll be, ok?*" said Geraintus allowing the frail looking wizard to lean on him.

"*We need to get him home Molly,*" said Garibaldi wrapping up the last of the holes the antennae had made. At least he'd stopped bleeding.

"*The dogs are coming back with some news, I think?*" said Tudor desperate for them to hurry. He needed to stay alive; he had spells to revoke, on his return to his partner. He felt a wave of nausea engulf him again as he tried to shake his guilt.

"*Wait Slobbers, they might have found a different way out, I may need to change the plan,*" said Molly.

Garibaldi with Tudor and Geraintus rushed towards the barking. Molly and the cats followed. Ivor sat with Bedivere; he was feeling just as frail.

Covered in thick cobwebs, ivy and overgrown debris was indeed an outline of an exit door.

"*Oh my, this is good news,*" said Molly getting excited. "*Millie, can you clear it?*"

"*Datrys ar unwaith/ Dah Treece arh eenwaheeth,*" as she swished her tail three times. Molly had taught her well.

The door was heavily disguised and part of the brick passage, oak and heavy but with no apparent handle.

Slobbers, Fabbles were quick to take a closer look.

"It'll take me much longer to open this Molly, if at all. There's no apparent edge, but we can try," said Slobbers.

"Geraintus, can you take a look, as there's a tiny gap at the top," said Molly astute and thinking fast.

Geraintus moved closer and there was a small slit above, enough for him to peer out and see what was in front of the door.

"What can you see?" asked Garibaldi wishing they could leave soon; he was getting anxious.

"It's facing the fields behind the castle. The coach is behind the cluster of oak trees as is Harry. If I whistle, he's within hearing distance," said Geraintus excited. Before anyone could say anything he then exclaimed,

"Oh no, there's a dozen sentry men outside too, all gathered round, and Thomas Beckett is with them. I thought we'd drugged him 'til Christmas. He must be telling the sentry that we're in here and that we're trying to steal the coracle."

Ginger One appeared as Geraintus relayed this news.

"I can add more problems to that."

"What's the status?" asked Molly trying to think twice as fast.

"They must presume you'll find this secret door," said Ginger One, *"But there's a castle full of problems. The Croggs are on their way with another hundred bug*

dogs, they're over the horizon but will be here shortly. There's sentry all around the castle, every ten to twelve feet and they've spears but also bludgeons and armour."

Everyone stood still and appeared shocked at this news.

"We will split up; this is what we'll do. At no point does anyone wait for me, or each other. Once out of here, our objective was as before, we must get to the coach and leave," instructed Molly as Bedivere started to feel faint. He wasn't sure if he could walk out of the dungeon let alone make it to the coach. Millie felt this and asked,

"Can we not spell the coach to come closer in invisible mode?" asked Millie again.

"No, we're losing spell capacity. We must save our spells until we need them to kill the enemy when we leave. There's not much time; this is what we'll do.

Fabbles, nip out and scour the castle as Ginger One will be recognised by Beckett's closest sentries as a Llewellyn cat. You can go about less detected. Check the exit points and see where the Croggs are in relation to our timing to leave. Slobbers start on that brick door, whilst we decide how we're going to split up," instructed Molly as Slobbers jumped on it as Wibbly and Millie assisted in finding the actual edges and latch if there was one.

Fabbles disappeared and Garibaldi paled as he wasn't going to like this bit, he just had that feeling.

"Right, we'll create two diversions, and the third party will carry the coracle to the cart. Send a spell with a pebble to Harry, Gari. Tell him to continue with the cart being cloaked as this is crucial for our get away. Once he's in place and Fabbles is back, we'll leave."

Ivor was fidgeting as was Tudor. Bedivere was weak and Geraintus sat next to him propping him up until he knew what he was doing next. Yo-Yo inside Geraintus' shirt was horrified to hear they were all going to split up.

"Fabbles is back," Garibaldi muttered. "He's making quicker progress than we all thought. Wibbly has found the join, which gives us the size of the door. We can in fact take the coracle out that way as it's wide enough."

"I think they're expecting you to go out that way. There are more guards and sentries outside the dungeon wall area."

"What about the twin towered gatehouse?"

"The gates are open and there are several horses grazing outside that belong to the sentries, I think. I've seen Harry he's grazing with the horses and he's wearing a brown and white saddle for us to remember. He's also changed colour and is chestnut to blend in with the others," reported Fabbles grinning. "He's a few yards away from the main group but his cart is hidden and doesn't want the others near it."

"Good, this is what we'll do," said Molly as they gathered round.

"Geraintus, Gari and Tudor, you must carry the coracle. I will go in front as look out with Ivor. Bedivere you're not able to carry the coracle, you'll come with me, and Ivor and we will keep you moving. Slobbers, you, and Ginger One will unpick the lock and Millie; you will bark and make noises to make sure the men believe you're going to come out of that door.

Fabbles once they realise you've defected; they'll hate you as much as want to kill me; therefore, you'll go to the fifth storey of the tower porch with Wibbly Alf. Make sure you're spotted as if you're trying to escape. Hopefully, this will keep them all busy, between the door to be opened and spotting you on the tower porch, this should divert them from the gate house entrance."

"What happens if the gate house is closed?"

"Geraintus, I'm going ahead of you, I will deal with it. Also, Wibbly can pebble me with anything he might think we need to know on the ground," reassured Molly.

"I've got to split us all up, as the links in our collars and chains are all effective. If one doesn't get back to the coach, then the rest remaining will have enough links to marry the coracle to the spoon."

A heavy silence went through the dungeon at this comment, but this was very real, they were under threat.

"Let me start our safe spell. We will have around forty minutes from the time we leave here to the coach everyone. I shall spell the dungeon door for you Slobbers in order you can get out that way, I know it's the longest *route, but the choice is yours. No one will be able to lock you in once we've gone. Are we ready?"*

"*Encarna lerin, encarna lerin,*" she whispered several times. She swished her tail in the air scattering angel dust over the whole dungeon as everyone spluttered shook themselves down and got ready for action.

Geraintus heaved the coracle on his own as Tudor and Gari took one side. Molly went ahead with Ivor and Bedivere both frail in the middle and left the dungeon quickly. Molly waved her tail at the door and spelled it safe for Slobbers, Ginger, and Millie.

"*They'll get out in time, won't they?*" said Bedivere very weak and unhappy.

"*They're fitter than everyone, they've got time to run round the long way and be attacked and have as much chance as us, Bedivere. We must think positive and move quickly, come on.*"

***

"*Have they seen us yet?*" asked Wibbly who was perched on the tower porch for everyone to see as he watched the men patrolling the perimeter.

"*Not sure Wibbly, but we must look as if we're hiding and not providing a diversion,*" giggled Fabbles who was having a wonderful time.

"*Yes, they have,*" Wibbly Alf ducked from an arrow heading his way.

"*Fabbles, they're attacking.*"

Fabbles crouched down on the ground completely hidden and focussed on the gatehouse to warn Molly if necessary. Wibbly couldn't hide as well and moved around the porch trying to avoid the windows. The spears were firing in all directions and Fabbles thought, the more they threw, the less they had for later, for when they had to make a dash for it.

Suddenly there was commotion of a different kind as Fabbles witnessed that the warriors below had realised that there was noise coming from inside the dungeon. This made the sentries stand guard outside and Wibbly knew that they'd no chance escaping through that door. They'd be killed instantly. He couldn't bear the thought of losing Millie, having found her. He kept his head down as the arrows continued to fly over them. Fabbles and he both saw Kentav Crogg turn up again and a hundred or so bug dogs started to crawl over the castle.

***

Millie was perched on Gingers' shoulders and could see out of the gap on top of the door, which was certainly coming apart from the wall, albeit very slowly.

"The bug dogs are back, I can see Kentav's tall hat, and they're here all right. You're not really opening this door, Slobbers?"

"Yes and no," said Slobbers, with his claw inside the rusty old latch which they'd discovered earlier. *"This is the shortest route back to the coach."*

"Yes, and the most dangerous," said Millie jumping from Gingers' shoulders.

"Why don't we make our way back now, the same way as the wizards? They know we're here; we don't need to stay any longer," said Ginger. *"It'll give us a chance to get to the coach and not be left behind."*

"We still need to run round the castle walls to the church as the coach is behind the cluster of oak trees, near it. We might as well try the shortest route if we're going to get attacked."

Millie wasn't entirely happy with this statement from Slobbers, she was worried about Wibbly.

"Are we going to wait for Wibbly and Fabbles to get away to the coach first?"

"No chance, we'll all run out together, even if we run from here. It'll be the same time. I've already given Fabbles the signals; don't worry," as he picked the lock with more gusto than before.

Ginger and Millie looked at each other, both worried. They'd some protection spell but not enough to outrun the enemy and get to the coach.

***

"The bug dogs are all over the inside of the castle, Molly," whispered Ivor as they all walked as close to the curtain wall carrying the coracle. Bedivere was holding on to Ivor and both were moving quickly to Molly's relief.

"Let's keep to the wall as much as we can. We need to quicken our pace and hope that the Begglys haven't tried the dungeon door yet."

A pebble dropped into Ivor's hand as they continued. Geraintus was puffing behind them with Tudor and Gari carrying the coracle as close to the wall as they could.

"The gate house is closing, we must hurry," Ivor said reading Fabbles' pebble.

"I'll go," said Bedivere suddenly quickening his pace. He went round the corner to be struck by three bug dogs in the chest as he fell to the ground.

"Etnaskillen gianto, Etnaskillen gianto," shouted Molly as she spun her tail three times, killing the three bug dogs as they rolled over, with their electronic round legs in the air. She opened the gatehouse and didn't hesitate to summon Harry with one spin of her tail. Bedivere groaned on the floor as Garibaldi rushed to his aid with Ivor. Tudor who was panting and red in the face was determined to keep up with Geraintus.

"Hurry Ivor, Gari take Bedivere to the cart. Geraintus come on, we must get out as there are more bug dogs on their way," commanded Molly swishing angel dust over everyone.

"On three, we must all run at once."

The outline of the cart was visible to them alone. Bedivere was burning, his cloak was on fire as Gari waved his hand over him, dampened the cloak, but he was very weak. He knew he had to run as he got up, with Ivor assisting him.

Molly led the way, there were no apparent bug dogs in their path as suddenly the spears started to fly towards them in substantial numbers.

"Quick everyone," she encouraged and showered them all with angel dust.

One spear caught Geraintus in the arm as he grunted but continued to carry the coracle. Tudor petrified as was Garibaldi hurried towards Harry. As they neared, Kentav Crogg appeared from nowhere, nearly bumping into Molly with thirty bug dogs who surrounded them in three seconds flat.

"Put the coracle down," commanded Kentav pleased with this sudden scoop.

"No Kentav, it belongs to the Llewellyn family, and you know it," said Molly defiant and determined. They'd come this far; the cart was a few yards away and she could spell them away....

Zzzzzzzzzz............

The bug dogs swirled their antennae towards the party, singeing Gari's beard as he dropped his end of the coracle to put out the flame. Geraintus was hit yet again and before Molly could retaliate.... Tudor dropped his corner of the coracle and walked towards Kentav.

"Etnaskillen gianto, Etnaskillen gianto," he shouted and waved his arm. His flamed cloak reacted as he

stormed towards Kentav to give Molly and the others a chance to leave with the coracle.

Tudor fell to the ground in front of Bedivere who was barely standing. They all knew, even Molly that there was no hope in staying alive if they moved. The coracle now on the ground started to fidget.

"Seize the coracle," shouted Kentav as the bug dogs squared up to the remaining family standing as Molly didn't move; her tail erect waiting for an opportunity to retaliate.

The Llewellyn's stood and watched the Crogg army lift the coracle and walk towards the church tower. Kentav, who was bursting with power and confidence stated,

"You can go, we only want the coracle as we've got the spoon," he chuckled.

Garibaldi and Geraintus looked at Molly in horror as Ivor paled and was about to drop to his knees to check on Tudor. No one was sure if this was a blatant lie or did, he really have the spoon? Molly felt dreadful as she wasn't sure where the spoon was hidden by Yo-Yo and what had happened to him? For someone in charge of everyone she hadn't really done a decent job. Ivor was inconsolable as he got up and muttered that Tudor was dead. Molly shook herself back to the moment.

"Get in the cart; we must make our way back towards the trees. We might as well keep a safe distance back but watch where he's going to take the coracle. He can't move that fast, they're not interested in us,"

said Molly as Bedivere hanging on to Ivor went ahead. Geraintus tried to fix his wounds nodded as Garibaldi tried to move Tudor.

"Leave him Gari we can't take him," said Molly knowing their spells couldn't carry a dead wizard.

Shocked but he didn't argue Garibaldi went ahead with Geraintus.

***

Wibbly Alf and Fabbles looked down in horror from the fifth storey tower porch as the Llewellyn's were being attacked and surrounded by the Croggs. They saw Tudor being killed and they knew they had to do something fast.

"Can you jump into the coracle Fabbles? I know its high from here, but can you unsteady the Croggs? Jump in and jump out again and make a run for the coach. They'll be passing under us in a minute. Just to confuse them a bit."

"Yes of course, but what about you?"

"The gatehouse is still open, and Molly and the others are walking behind the Croggs, look. Harry is walking a few paces to their side. I'm going to make a dash for it and join them."

"What about Ginger, Slobbers and Millie?"

"Fabbles, they're going to make their own way. They need your signal as you jump. They can decide how they're going to run for the coach, they'll have decided

on that already. We must all worry about ourselves right now. Go, jump, and call the signal."

Fabbles knew this was his moment as he prepared to make a flying leap into the coracle which was moving underneath him. He let out a loud screeching wail for Slobbers as he dived towards the coracle. Wibbly Alf didn't waste any time, he made his way quickly down the steps towards the gatehouse. He wanted to catch up with the family before anyone had noticed the gate house was open and furthermore; he wasn't going to be left behind.

***

"Let's spell them," said Ivor who was trying not to get emotional for losing his brother. He was more upset that they were leaving him on the ground for the Beggly army and Croggs to trample over him.

Molly looked behind her and then upwards towards the fifth tower. Harry was grazing and was slowly making his way towards them undetected. Tudor lay dead covered in his red cloak and ignored. Bedivere was being fixed again by Geraintus and Geraintus was being fixed by Garibaldi as they walked at a safe distance from the Croggs.

"Fabbles is about to jump onto the coracle Ivor. Start throwing spells when he hits it. He's going to create some havoc. We need to see if we can take it from them. Gari, Ivor spell them all, once Fabbles hits the deck. Geraintus, help me snatch the coracle we're yards from the coach."

No one had time to think as Fabbles spun in the air, wailing loudly to signal Slobbers as he threw himself tummy first into the coracle unsteadying all the little Croggs who were carrying it. The Croggs went flying everywhere and the coracle toppled over, but with Fabbles underneath it.

Geraintus and Molly were there in a second and Harry the horse came up behind kicking the Croggs. Wibbly Alf started to spin his tail attacking the few bug dogs who had noticed the incident which had been behind them. The bug dog leaders were all dead and without Kentav's direct orders they were disorientated and could only spin round and round sparking their antennae, hoping to hit the odd wizard.

Ivor continued to shower his spell at the party as Wibbly and Harry killed a few Croggs whilst Molly tried to turn the coracle with Gari.

"Bedivere get to the coach, Gari you too. I'll deal with this," shouted Molly over the wailing coming from under it. Wibbly came up quickly to assist and attached his link chain to the coracle and it flipped over. Fabbles was squashed but all right. Wibbly threw him in the coracle and with Molly dragged it towards the coach, a few feet away as a spear hit Harry and he fell to the ground.

"RUN," shouted Molly.

"Turn it upside down, it will protect us, until we get inside the coach," said Ivor knowing there was no way they could get back to collect Tudor or Elijas.

Ivor, Molly and Geraintus started to run with the coracle over their heads with Wibbly attached to its chain. Fabbles was slightly concussed and was being held up by Wibbly as they ran. They reached the corner of the church tower to see the coach ahead, floating inconspicuously with the glass steps swaying waiting for them to climb up immediately.

"*STOP,*" ordered a dozen sentry men with spears and bludgeons.

"*So close,*" thought Molly thinking fast.

"*Thomas Beckett has informed us that this coracle belongs to the Croggs. Release it or take the consequences. We've orders to kill you,*" said the leader.

As the sentry man towered over them and as they were partially hidden by the coracle; Molly could see Millie, Slobbers and Ginger creep out of the dungeon door and were now behind the sentry men with no bug dogs or Croggs in sight. They were still concussed or killed from Fabbles dive bomb. The few that had survived the dive bomb were disorientated and taking their time to re-group to attack.

Molly nodded at Millie, and they knew what they were to do. Geraintus moved away as he was too tall, and the sentry nodded. Slowly they all moved away from the coracle. Wibbly unlinked himself from the chain as the sentry men satisfied, went over to take it from them. Wibbly grabbed Fabbles who was looking rather delicate and still too unsteady to run on his own.

Bedivere, Gari and Ivor, now in the coach watched. The Croggs were coming up behind Molly as she walked away with Geraintus, Fabbles and Wibbly.

The Croggs caught up with the sentry men and started clapping each other on the back as Millie, Ginger and Slobbers joined Molly. They made their way to the coach, watching the Croggs and men congratulate themselves on their victory.

"Millie, its time," said Molly hoping their idea would work as they were within jumping distance of the coach. Geraintus towered over them all and suddenly before Millie could cast her spell a razor-sharp purple light appeared from Geraintus' tunic and Yo-Yo appeared shouting,

"TAKE COVER," as he rolled into a ball and flung himself into the air, his overlarge studded collar acting as a spinning wheel.

"Nooo," shouted Molly knowing it was too late.

Yo-yo jumped in the air and in a tight black furry ball, with his larger-than-life studded collar flew a hundred miles an hour towards the Croggs, warriors and bug dogs. In an instant it was all over.

He blew himself and all the knights, Croggs and creatures around the coracle into thousands of little pieces.

***

There was no time to comprehend what had just happened. Through the thick purple smoke Molly,

Millie, and Slobbers picked up the Colden Coracle and ran to the waiting coach, as the coach zoomed out of view the minute the last paw jumped inside.

Chapter 5

The Hugglett Spoon

There was a hush inside the coach as they realised what Yo-Yo had done. On the dashboard of the three feathers coach, as it flew towards the whispering fig tree, was the miners' lantern. It was silently spewing colourless smoke and next to it was the hovel, twitching. Geraintus was attending yet again to Bedivere's wounds and Ivor had cut Garibaldi's' beard clean away as it had been burnt in several places.

The animals were unscathed as Fabbles recovered quickly as he and Slobbers sat in the coracle; with Wibbly and Millie side by side, pleased to be safe. Ginger One kept checking the two lockets around his neck, he couldn't wait to give Ginger Two his. There was another one, which Molly hadn't said much about. He'd ask her later.

Ivor and Molly were trying to focus. The mere fact they'd left Tudor, Elijas, and Harry behind hadn't been a choice. Molly was hoping that Kentav Crogg had been blown up with his army. However, something told her, that he'd survived the onslaught of Yo-Yo. The sooner they collected the spoon, the quicker they could move to Castell Coch with the treasures and marry them with the treasure chest.

To get the others out of the trance they were in with the shock of Yo-Yo's actions, Molly decided to relay the poem he'd left to get them all focussed on the task in hand.

"Let's find the spoon," said Molly, *"This was what Yo-Yo left under the lantern;* **"Kayealexaly, Kayealexaly, free us to our family, Huggle-Puggle we're not trouble, whispering fig tree is now white, Golden Coracle mustn't have a fright. Wake up to Kayealexaly.""**

"Are we going to the tree?" asked Millie.

"Yes, we need to see if it turns white, he must have hidden the spoon there," said Molly. *"I need your help everyone as I'm not truly sure it's there. However, we must eliminate it before we head back to Narberth."*

"Can we not move the cave back to Saundersfoot?" asked Fabbles.

"No, we need to keep it moving as the Croggs are still searching for the spoon and of course, now we've taken the coracle, they'll want a bigger battle."

"What about our brother," asked Ginger.

"He's safe inside the cave, wherever the cave is located don't worry," said Gari.

"We've lost family members today, but we mustn't forget we've gained some too," said Ivor trying to lighten the mood by avoiding his own grief.

Fabbles and Ginger both spun their tails in the air in acknowledgment and Gari and Molly started to feel the focus returning.

"We're nearing the tree," whispered Geraintus as he looked over at Bedivere who was indeed very frail.

White froth started to flow out of the lantern and the hovel started to screech as the coach flew lower in the direction of Geraintus' back garden.

"Ivor keep watch on the hovel and Gari stay here. Geraintus and Bedivere sit in the coracle. We'll find the spoon. Keep hovering over us and I'll signal if you're to leave. If you see any Croggs, fly immediately to Narberth, collect Ginger, and fly to Castell Coch. Wibbly, we need you linked to the coracle with that chain, which is the key to the spoon. You'll need to stay here," instructed Molly as the cats got ready to jump from the coach with her.

With a swish of her tail, the glass doors opened, the steps shot out of the belly, and they jumped out.

The coach hovered above.

"Millie start digging and moving around under the left side. Slobbers, Fabbles climb the tree and look on every branch for a clue. We can't use spells as Yo-Yo has spelled the area for us to find the spoon by paw. Look for a white collar or a white marker, anything that looks out of place. Hold on tight as the tree will be wondering what we're suddenly up to."

Molly realised that Yo-Yo had had a white collar and suddenly she remembered she hadn't seen it for a while. She started murmuring spells around the tree, opposite to Millie and they got to work, searching.

"I think I have something," called Fabbles who was in the middle of the tree.

"Describe it."

"It's a white collar with a turquoise studded stone in the middle. It's hanging over a thick branch and partially hidden."

"That's it, Fabbles, bring it down gently," instructed Molly as Millie stopped searching. Slobbers came down the top branches very quickly, he clearly remembered the last time he was up this tree. Molly summoned the coach to return with a swish of her bushy tail and the glass steps stumbled out of the side before Fabbles got down with the collar in his mouth.

"Quick, inside, we must leave at once," said Molly who realised that this was Yo-Yo's instruction where the spoon was hidden and not the location.

"Where to?" asked Ivor who'd lost the plot and had started to age dramatically with worry.

"Nowhere yet, we need to read this message first," said Garibaldi realising that Ivor needed a strong spell potion the minute he got back inside the cave.

Molly opened the parchment and quickly scanned it but decided it needed to be read aloud,

"Dear Molly,

If you're reading this, I hope you're all recovered by what I've done. My only mission was to save the Llewellyn family and you from the Croggs. Forgive me for disobeying orders but the spoon is safe and can be

retrieved in your cave in Narberth with Ginger Two. Ginger Two doesn't realise that the cushion I gave him to rest his injured paw holds the Hugglett spoon. It can be opened by his locket, which you'll have in your possession from the Golden Coracle.

Merlin had informed me of the brothers, I'm so pleased they've found each other. Whatever happens from the time I instigated this, only that locket will open the cushion.

Thank you for the opportunity of being with you all, the Llewellyn's and I shall think of you in Castell Coch from heaven.

Forgive me,

Your ever-loyal servant."

Yo-Yo.

"Narberth coach at once," summoned Garibaldi trying to brush a tear from his eye as everyone fell silent.

"What about Saundersfoot?" asked Bedivere.

"It's in outline mode Bedivere. If the Croggs march towards it, they'll not realise until they're at the front door that it isn't there. We've lights coming on and off at various times of the day. It looks as if we're in," chuckled Gari as Bedivere smiled but shut his eyes again.He felt rather exhausted by it all.

"Wibbly, I suggest you keep yourself attached to the coracle until we make Narberth safe. We'll be travelling to Castell Coch in the morning."

"Why can't we go straight there, once we've collected Ginger and the spoon?" asked Millie.

"Hopkin Paulinus has instructed us that whatever happens we can only approach Castell Coch in daylight because of the Eagles."

"I thought he was there in advance to sort them out, surely we're not expecting two Eagles to dictate to us about what's ours," said Ivor exasperated with it all.

"Ivor, quite frankly you haven't been exactly forthcoming with all your knowledge to date. Hopkin Paulinus is reassuring two Golden Eagles, who have protected your treasure and all the papers inside, from Croggs and other enemies. Surely, you can see that," said Garibaldi frustrated with his master and was losing patience.

"Enough," said Molly. *"Hopkin Paulinus will let us know when the Castle is ready for us. We don't want to be flying in over the walls upsetting Eagles. Currently we can only use the dangerous ravine on the forestry side. Hopkin does know best on this occasion Ivor."*

Wibbly and Millie were quiet and even the cats could feel that Ivor; head of the family, was obviously holding back on secrets. Slobbers knew them all and he thought that maybe when they got to Castell Coch, he would tell Molly. She'd helped him find his brothers, the least he could do, even things that Gari didn't want to talk about. Yes, he'd do that, he would tell her everything.

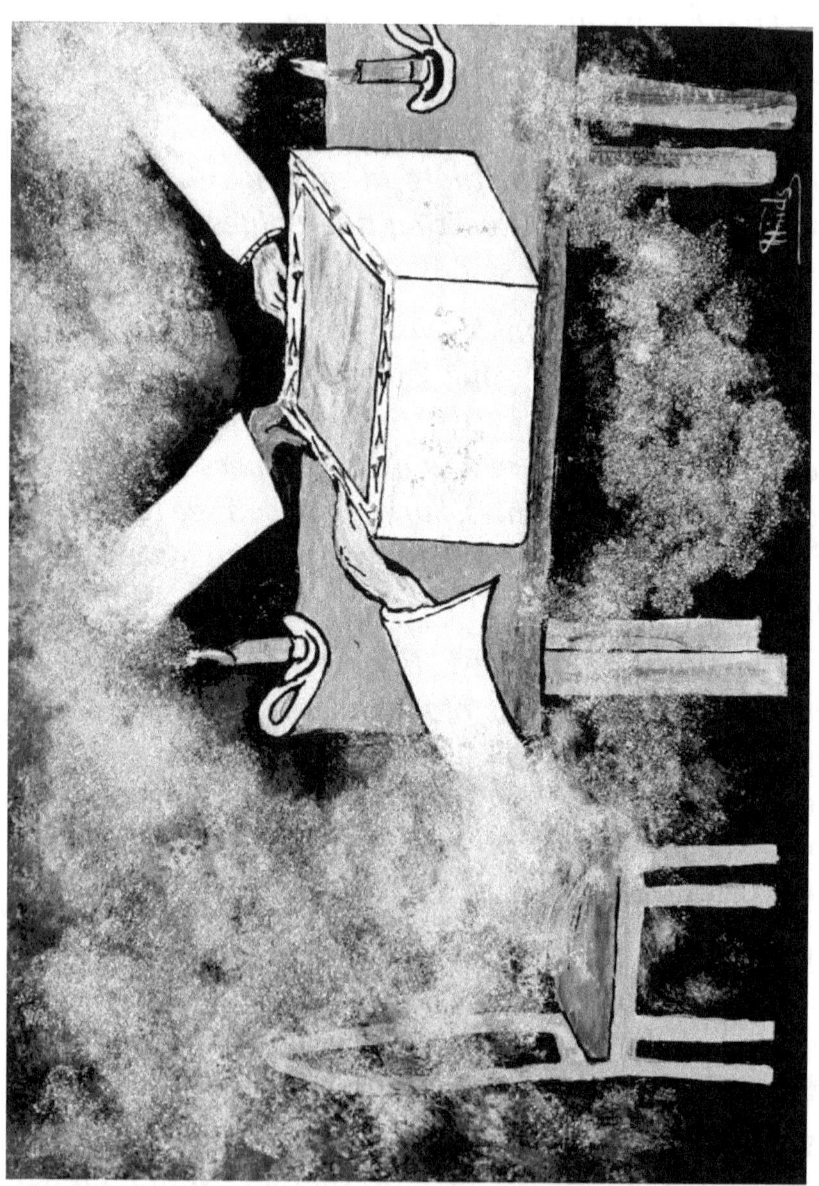

The Mystical hovel

He mustn't forget to tell her about that white puppy. Slobbers guessed Gari had erased that from his mind or had simply forgotten as it had been a long time ago. He wanted a plan also to find the fifth brother, once all this was over.

Plop, plop, plop.

"Fabbles, go with Slobbers and open the hovel, Gari get out the plans of the castle. We can look over them whilst we get to Narberth," instructed Molly who recognised that there were more past historical issues within the family. Ivor was certainly not forthcoming with the information. Ivor was either ashamed or had simply forgotten as his powers were dwindling.

"Pebbles from Hopkin," said Geraintus.

"That was quick, what does he say," asked Gari rearranging the dash of the coach to accommodate the hovel, maps, and papers.

Screeeeeeeeeeeech.

The hovel went nuts as it opened the inside of the cave at Narberth, something was afoot.

"Oh my," whispered Gari before Geraintus had a chance to relay the message. With this the miners' lantern started to churn out pink smoke, followed by black and a mixture of white and blacker smoke. Garibaldi was waving his hands, muttering spells under his breath as he continued to scrutinise the cave as Molly spoke.

"Gari wait, Geraintus, what's the message from Hopkin?" asked Molly getting frustrated.

"Don't waste a moment; leave at once. Crogg army on way to Saundersfoot."

"Why Saundersfoot?" asked Fabbles getting confused not yet understanding the Llewellyn codes.

"I agreed with Hopkin we would refer to the cave at Saundersfoot in case the pebbles got intercepted. I presume we have trouble in Narberth, Gari?"

"Yes, we've a problem. Ginger Two is hiding in the larder of the kitchen. There's one warrior inside, sitting by the fireplace. There are two warriors outside the front door."

"Where's the cushion can you see it?" asked Molly praying this was not going to be another disaster.

"Yes, it's on the couch, where the warrior is sitting. I've got an unobstructed view from here."

"We can't blame Ginger Two for not protecting the cushion. He wasn't made aware of its contents. We must rescue him and the cushion at once," said Molly.

"Let me see if I know them," said Ivor as he got up to join Gari at the dashboard.

"Coach get higher into clouds," instructed Molly. *"We'll wait for our moonbeam to encapsulate us and keep us spelled from harm. Once that descends on us, we'll agree together how to retrieve the spoon and Ginger,"* said Molly who had no idea at that precise moment.

She knew the plan would formulate in her mind; the minute the moonbeam covered them.

In the corner of the coach, Fabbles and Slobbers were in deep discussion as was Wibbly and Millie. Molly knew that within a few minutes, there'd be an idea forthcoming. Slobbers was more concerned than usual as this was his brother in imminent danger and he'd the key to unlock everything. His brother unknowingly needed to save the family.

⊷⊷⊲❖⊳⊶⊶

Chapter 6

Owain Glyndwr

I t seemed like four hours and not four minutes by the time the moonbeam hit the communication feathers of the coach. It struck with such force that everyone fell over as the coach tried to steady itself from the sharp blast.

"*At last,*" said Gari who fell headlong into the coracle and landed in-between Fabbles and Slobbers who found this amusing as their fur provided him with a soft landing.

The parchment holding the moonbeam message was of a chocolate colour and looked very official and it was secured with a turquoise and pink silk ribbon.

"*This is unusual,*" said Ivor as he got up from falling into Bedivere and Geraintus. "*Owain Glyndwr is the only warrior in these parts to have the right to send purple ribboned moonbeams, it should be good news,*" smiled Ivor, pleased it was direct from him.

"*Let's see then,*" said Molly and hoped he was right and had a plan in mind suddenly.

"*The cave has been intercepted in Saundersfoot; the outline has been destroyed. I trust you receive this prior to your arrival in Narberth. If anyone receives you there, it will not be an ally, tread carefully and good luck.*"

Her heart sank, there would have to be another battle of sorts. She composed herself but Gari was ahead of her as he could see she was exhausted by trying to think ahead all the time.

"Right," he said. *"Slobbers and Fabbles, you've been concocting something since we got in the coach, what's your plan?"*

"We'll use the secret passageway, creep into the cave, and go straight to the larder to rescue Ginger. Tell him everything and get him out first," said Slobbers.

"I'll stay put in case they've seen a cat in the cave," continued Fabbles.

"What then?" asked Ivor who didn't sound too impressed.

"While we're talking to Ginger, Bedivere and Geraintus can walk up to the cave door. They can pretend that Bedivere is more injured than he is and that they're returning by foot. The Croggs have got away with the coracle. They've also successfully killed Molly and all the Llewellyn family.

This will distract them inside and Geraintus can get to the larder, help open a window to let us all out and Bedivere can throw the cushion on the floor, while he says he's poorly. I'll creep in, get it, and bring it back to the larder," said Fabbles anxious to prove what an asset he was going to be working with Slobbers.

"Simple and could work," said Molly, *"But I should go instead of you."*

"No Molly. I think it's a clever idea that they think you've perished in that battle. It might give us an advantage as we're still unsure if Kentav's alive after that blast," said Geraintus.

"How do we escape?" asked Bedivere not really wanting to do this, but he did want his own castle. He was very fond of Geraintus and if he was with him, then he'd feel safe.

"Through the secret passage or Molly will open the kitchen window the minute you need it. We'll spell you back in but be prepared for a rough landing into the coracle. You'll be catapulted through the moonbeam," smiled Gari.

"Ivor extend the hovel and make room around the window; we'll be prepared here. We shall monitor your moves and if Gari inserts double pins on your person, we can issue instructions to you as well as watch both rooms at the same time," said Molly eager for this to work.

Gari placed double pins on the two cats, Geraintus and Bedivere. Ivor astonished everyone by spelling injuries all over Geraintus and Bedivere felt quite sick. He looked even worse for wear than he felt earlier. With Geraintus by his side, he would be fine. He convinced himself of this but knew it was time to get on with it.

"Don't forget Geraintus, Bedivere. You must visibly relax once you're in the cave. Let them think you trust them," instructed Gari feeling nervous all of a sudden for them.

Molly swished her tail in the air three times and angel dust scattered over everyone as the coach opened its communication feathers on command. The coach hovered a few feet from the ground and a mile from the cave as the two cats disappeared away from the area to enter through the secret passageways.

Geraintus and Bedivere left via the steps and made their way towards the cave. Bedivere was bleeding profusely from one wound, which Geraintus had only fixed an hour earlier. Geraintus had several deep open wounds also, which made him appear worse than Bedivere. Bedivere leant on the giant as they made their way down the long path. It was important to behave in such a way as the two warriors by the front door had already noticed them limping wearily towards them. They disappeared inside.

The coach hovered above in a silk fluffy cloud which blended in with the other clouds and floated aimlessly above. Molly got to work as soon as the coach went inside the clouds. She threw her tail out of the communication hatch which was purposely left ajar. This was to assist Gari in receiving the conversation from the double pins.

"Agor ar unwaith, benialli, benialli/ Ahgor ah eenwaheeth, ben-eealee, ben-eealee," instructed Molly as the kitchen window of the cave silently opened upwards.

Everyone in the coach held their breath as Gari watched the hovel and checked that no one had heard the window open.

Rat, Tat.

Geraintus knocked on the cave door. The cave door creaked open, and the warrior looked at a bleeding green giant and an equally bloody wizard who looked half dead.

"Who comes here?" the warrior spoke with a thick accent.

"Let us in quick," said Geraintus in a loud agitated voice propping Bedivere up more than he needed to. He pushed passed the warrior and went inside to the front room.

"What is it?" asked the other warrior. All three warriors were now gathered round Geraintus and Bedivere. Bedivere was helped on to the couch and Geraintus sat next to him bleeding all over the place.

"We've escaped from a huge battle, let us sit and explain," said Geraintus as he threw the cushion away to the floor. He was breathing so heavily the curtains at the windows were swaying back and forth as the cushion landed further away from the couch area.

"Can you go into the kitchen and find me some potions, I must stop this bleeding otherwise Bedivere is going to perish," instructed Geraintus deliberately breathing heavy making the warriors move away slightly.

Apart from one warrior, the other two looked very alarmed and went to the kitchen to look for a potion or two. Thankfully, Ginger Two had already realised that something was happening as he'd seen the window open. He'd hidden himself in the sacking of wheat which was inside the cupboard on the floor. His coat blended in nicely with the light ginger sack and he'd covered himself with Gari's aprons to be sure.

"They're back," he thought as he hid and listened to the man rustling around in the cupboards with no idea what Geraintus needed.

They returned to the living room as the blood continued to pour from both giant and wizard, making the warriors uncomfortable.

"We've no idea what you need. Feel free to find what potions are necessary for you both to stop the bleeding," said the warrior as the second one went to stand by the front door. It was obvious they were not going to allow them to leave.

Geraintus pleased with this kicked the cushion even further away and it landed behind the living room door. He couldn't pick it up but waited. He found what he needed, winked at Ginger, hiding in the cupboard and as he towered in the doorway he smiled as he let Fabbles, and Slobbers slip past him into the kitchen.

The stench of the potions that Geraintus was smothering all over Bedivere, which was truly unnecessary, was dreadful. So much so, the warriors turned their back on the giant as he administered the sticky stench on Bedivere. Bedivere wanted to pass out genuinely as the potion was truly disgusting.

"What happened," asked one of them eventually.

"Who are you and why are you in Ivor's cave," asked Geraintus stalling.

"I apologise," said the tallest warrior standing by the fireplace. *"I'm part of Owain Glyndwr's army. We've come to see Ivor and check that you all survived the battle, the one we were told about this morning."*

"You can see it was a bloody mess out there," elaborated Geraintus who now administered the dreadful stuff to his own wounds. Bedivere lay motionless on the sofa, the stench from the potion made him feel genuinely ill, there was no need to fake it.

***

In the three feathers coach, they all watched and listened to what was being said. Molly was ready to spell their return through the secret passageway if necessary.

***

"The Croggs and Thomas Beckett's army attacked us at Llawhaden Castle; they've taken the Golden Coracle from us. Bedivere was hit several times as was I. Tudor and all the family, even the Magical Molly have gone. We've lost everyone," said Geraintus his voice breaking as he manufactured large green tears which rolled from his eyes as he continued to look down at his wounds,

administering the smelly potion. Bedivere watched him in amazement.

On this information the warrior looked at his colleague, they huddled and whispered and one of them went outside to talk to the main warrior. Whilst they were in a huddle Fabbles crept behind the sofa. Geraintus watched him and stood up towering over the men as Fabbles quickly got the cushion back to the kitchen.

"Good," whispered Garibaldi from the top deck of the coach. *"We're down to two men, one of the warriors is marching off somewhere."*

"Probably to tell Kentav Crogg, that we've been blown up," said Molly now convinced he was still alive.

The only warrior remaining returned to the fireplace as Geraintus heaved his bulky frame on the couch next to Bedivere who was feeling ill, the stench of the potion being quite unbearable.

"We'd heard that you'd all survived," said the warrior who looked a bit agitated.

"I'd like to know where they are then," said Geraintus.

"We appeared dead on the field as did the others, when we thought it safe, none of the others moved when we tried to leave. The dogs including Molly were all in bits over the field. One of our own dogs had used his own spells and blew us all up," croaked Bedivere thinking best be closer to the truth as they obviously knew more than they were telling.

This satisfied the warrior by the fireplace.

"I suggest you tell Owain everything as he'll be coming later to talk to you. Don't be offended but my orders are to keep you both here until he arrives."

As the warrior spoke, Geraintus could hear a noise coming from the kitchen as being a giant he had acute hearing. He guessed Slobbers and Fabbles were moving the cushion through the window. Geraintus sneezed so loudly at this point the whole cave shuddered which gave the three cats' the perfect opportunity to leave with the cushion to the awaiting coach.

"As soon as they're on the window sill Gari, shout as I'll spell them to the coach," said Molly as she prepared herself.

"Atishooooooooooooo," Geraintus sneezed loudly.

The three cats were through the window and jumped underneath it. They placed the cushion in the middle of their three tummies, hooked their tails together and whispered together,

"Kayealexaly, Kayealexaly."

With this Molly's spell kicked in and they were whisked in an instant towards the coach, which was purring and hovering in the silver cloud overhead. They tumbled into the coach, the cushion falling straight into the coracle; where Millie's instructions were to grab it, hold it tight until the hatch was safely closed.

Geraintus knowing the cats were safe winked at Bedivere and stroked his arm, which was a code between them.

" In that case, if we're to wait for Owain, I'll go and sleep in Ivor's room," said Bedivere croaking and sounding very feeble.

"I'll go and sleep in Molly's room. If I may make myself some more of this potion, I can administer it while I'm resting," said Geraintus. *"We're both weary after this awful battle, losing our treasure and our dear family. You can call us when Owain gets here."*

"Yes, get it on your way to rest," said the warrior glad the awful smell would disappear with his prisoners. He was pleased that keeping them here to wait for Kentav Crogg had been much easier than he'd envisaged.

"Send Geraintus the info now Gari as he goes into the kitchen," whispered Ivor as he helped Gari. Molly was busy telling the four cats their story in the coracle. The brothers certainly ecstatic to have found each other, Fabbles even more so. She promised to give them more information once they'd got to Castell Coch safely as they would want to find their fifth brother.

Wibbly sat with Millie on the outside of the coracle waiting for Gari's next instruction. Millie was on alert in case she needed to help get Bedivere and Geraintus to the coach.

"Stay there, Bedivere, I'll get some more potion and then I'll help you to Ivor's room," said Geraintus knowing

he was about to get a message from Garibaldi as per the plan.

Geraintus had no signal from Gari, he didn't worry. He went to get some more potions from the larder, checked the cats had disappeared, closed the window, and went to fetch Bedivere.

He nodded at the warrior who was glad he was leaving the room as the stench was heavy and lingered which made the man's eyes water. Geraintus dragged Bedivere to Molly's room and pretended to go to Ivor's room as he slammed the door, spelled it, and went to be with Bedivere. Geraintus wished Gari would hurry with the new instructions to leave by secret passageway as he had a grave feeling that Kentav Crogg was going to arrive much sooner rather than later.

Chapter 7

Cardiff Castle

"We need to link the treasures together quickly and get Geraintus out of the cave," instructed Molly.

"Shouldn't we get them out first?" said Millie.

"We haven't the power," Ivor whispered to Millie's disgust.

"Do you mean to say Geraintus and Bedivere weren't aware they may have to make their own way out of the cave, as they haven't enough powers of their own?"

"Yes, Millie they know. Geraintus is waiting for the sign. I can spell them back here but only from the secret passage. The problem is the passageways are no longer functional. It's nobody's fault. Quick, let Molly get the treasures together and then our powers will start to return," said Gari. *"Wibbly, unlink the chain and get on the dashboard to keep a look out for the Croggs. I'll help Molly."*

Wibbly disentangled himself from the coracle. The cats all jumped out as everyone turned to Molly. Ivor went to her side and brought his shepherds' stick which until now had been laying idle near the dashboard of the coach. The three feathers closed its communication hatch and secured the glass doors. All the double frosted glass covered the coach for more protection and suddenly it all became very real. The treasures were to be linked together in the silver cloud, above their temporary home, with enemy inside.

"Take your key from Slobbers Ginger Two, you have the honour of opening the cushion to let the spoon meet the Coracle for the first time in over a hundred years," commanded Molly as Ginger held the locket in his hand, already been given to him by an excited Slobbers. He didn't need to be told twice. He went immediately to the cushion which was placed on the ash seat. He opened the cushion and out slithered a silver and purple silk cloth with the spoon inside. Ginger One took the spoon out of its cover and handed it to Molly.

All the cats, Wibbly and Millie surrounded the coracle. Gari and Ivor stood side by side to Molly. The spoon sparkled and glowed, in turn the coracle started to move side to side its rich golden colour covering everyone in a golden shower of angel dust.

The spoon itself was a dark grey slate wearing several hundreds of little turquoise crystals which were sparkling as if on fire. The top part had woven hearts set in purple stones and below on its base was a crest of tiny moons all singing and dancing, which matched the love seat on the coracle. The candle emblem and quill were inscribed on the centre of the spoon next to rows of turquoise crystals. The ladle part of the spoon had hundreds of faintly engraved little half-moons all in a row below it.

There was a couple of hearts in between the main element which showed the green candle. There was an edge of gold throughout the long spoon, which was much heavier than they all anticipated. It mesmerised everyone for a full minute. The three links attached to the spoon was also slate. There was an additional long link chain attached to the spoon also.

"I Gorau Canwyll Pwyll, I Gorau Cannwyll Pwyll/ Ee ghor-ahee kah-noolth Poo-eelth," Molly whispered several times.

This was the first time Ivor had heard this spell for over a hundred years, and he'd forgotten that he must have told Molly, or she'd been briefed by Merlin. Nevertheless, they all stood still around the coracle.

Molly moved forward with the spoon in her paw and bowed at the coracle and handed the spoon to its link chain. It grabbed its treasure, and the spoon snapped closed to the link chain without fuss. The Golden Coracle seemed to sigh with relief and turned golden again as everyone cheered. The hovel screeched with full gusto making Gari jump over the coracle as did Wibbly to see what was wrong.

"Kentav Crogg is in the cave," he said. *"Geraintus and Bedivere need to leave now."*

"Shall we go?" asked Millie eager to get involved and help.

"Open the communication hatch Gari at once," commanded Ivor as Molly waved her tail in the air and waited for the coach to hover closer within their cloud.

"No Millie, we'll fly them home watch," said Molly as she felt her extra powers had arrived as quickly as the spoon had joined forces with the coracle.

***

Geraintus was trying not to get agitated as Bedivere was behaving as if he were truly injured and fragile and they'd only been pretending. He knew that Bedivere didn't have his full powers as he paced the room, waiting for Garibaldi's sign. He heard a noise and hoped that was the passageway being secretly opened but it was the front door.

His heart sank as he heard the shrill of Kentav's voice. There was no time to wait, they had to go to the secret passageway, risk being seen in the hallway, but they needed to get out right away. Then the pebble arrived.

***

Garibaldi was ready, as was Molly. He sent the pebble to Geraintus the minute he heard Kentav's awful shrill. Molly stood at the open coach window and swished her tail,

"Dewch adref ar unwaith, benialli, benialli/dehugh ah-drave ah-eenwaheeth, Beneealee, Beneealee," she repeated several times. An enormous gust of wind propelled the coach to spin round and round as everyone clutched the coracle for safety. Ivor fell upside down on the floor, his robes in the air as the coach kept spinning. Molly continued to chant.

Suddenly the gust of wind turned into a tornedo as Geraintus the green giant followed by a screaming Bedivere fell straight through the hatch headfirst onto Ivor. The coach slammed the hatch shut and purred upwards towards the safety of the second silver cloud as Gari laughed aloud and couldn't stop laughing for a good few minutes.

He was still laughing as everyone untangled themselves as Molly had collapsed briefly with the trance, exhausted.

The coach secured itself whilst it waited for new instructions. It gathered a dark cloud around it, to protect the family and its talons hovered within the cloud as in a floating stance. This position was to ensure all inside relaxed for a moment to give the treasures a few moments to adjust to being together again, for the first time in an extraordinarily long time.

***

Kentav had marched towards the main bedroom to interrogate the two Llewellyn's at the same second the enemy had disappeared in a flash of light. There was no sign of anyone apart from a heavy stench. He was as red as his orange tuft of hair as he asked Flynn,

"Where are they?"

He shouted at the top of his voice as it echoed above the clouds into the coach as everyone heard the commotion below and joined Gari in a little chuckle. Ivor took command for the very first time and ordered the coach towards Castell Coch.

Ivor sat down exhausted, and Molly rearranged herself with a clear view of everyone as Gari continued to watch the hovel. Molly could see everyone slumbering and she realised as she observed them all that they all wanted to live with her, but the castle wasn't big enough.

She'd read everyone's minds as they relaxed a little. The whole experience and obvious drama had knocked the energy out of them. However, she smiled and reminisced at the same time.

It was apparent that Wibbly Alf and Millie were an item and would want to be together. It was obvious to Molly the way Bedivere, who was sleeping against the chest of his hero Geraintus the giant had bonded too. That made it easier for her to make her next decisions. The cats were brothers, and they'd all have to be with Garibaldi. She thought about Gertrude, Harry, Elijas and Tudor and was sad for a moment. So many family members lost, just to re-unite the treasure. They still needed to unite the treasure chest.

She missed Yo-Yo more than she could say. He'd known her secret anguish and there was no one yet she felt she could confide in. Her mission wasn't complete, and she couldn't tell anyone until they were all safe in Castell Coch with all three treasures together.

She hoped it wasn't going to be too long before she felt able to confide in Garibaldi, Ivor and all the family. She would need their help for when the time came.

"Molly."

Garibaldi brought her back to the present as he handed a feather bound pebble to her which made her sit up immediately.

"We're not expecting to hear from Owain," as she opened the pebble.

"Re-direct to Cardiff Castle as Croggs en route to Castell Coch and will be there to ambush you. Make Cardiff safe. An army is on the way to Coch to assist. Eagles don't believe Hopkin Paulinus. Owain."

A gasp of horror went through the coach as Garibaldi went straight to the dash and re-directed the coach. It veered right sharply which threw the cats into the coracle once more, to everyone's amusement.

"Why can't we go and fight the Croggs. We're much stronger now?" asked Millie who was desperate to kill a few more of those little people, especially the Begglys.

"We've lost too many family members already. We shall secure Cardiff and tactically make a journey to Castell Coch once we've heard from Hopkin and Owain. There's simply too much risk turning up, with both treasures and lose them again," said Molly as everyone nodded. The grave facts were obvious. They'd lost too many members of family to date, and they wouldn't be effective with their numbers dwindling, even though their powers were returning.

"Once we get into Cardiff, we can all rest overnight and regain some powers from the treasures. We can then get to Castell Coch ready for a fight," said Ivor who suddenly felt more powerful than he'd felt in ages.

"Kentav Crogg needs something in that treasure chest, and someone has told him, where it is," said Gari looking at Molly and then Ivor who turned crimson.

"Whatever he wants, he's not giving up, which means if we wait until we've more information, we can attack better with a plan," said Molly again looking at Ivor. She wished he would tell her the crucial bit of the jigsaw which was missing. The animals felt better knowing at least Molly would not send them to fight unnecessarily.

Plonk, plonk, plop, plop

Two pebbles appeared at once through the hatch as Gari was quick to retrieve them.

"This one's from Hopkin, he says, "Confirm password, we need Ginger Two's locket to open treasure chest to release parchments of ownership. Eagles are to be released from duty once chest is open. Cavern only entrance, forestry deep water and dangerous, wait for instructions in Cardiff-Hopkin.""

"There's something in those papers that Kentav needs, Ivor. What is it?" demanded Molly losing patience with him for being silent.

"I've no idea," said Ivor not convincing anyone least of all Gari who opened the next pebble at once.

"This one's from Owain, "Crogg army and bug dogs surrounding parts of castle. We'll attack at dawn. Cavern only entrance, Treasure chest requires attention. Be aware.""

"Everyone seems to know that the treasure chest we need is at Castell Coch suddenly," said Wibbly as everyone agreed.

"We're outside Cardiff, at Penarth. We need to open the hovel and check for anything odd, before we fly to the castle," said Ivor as Gari went to the hovel to instigate a map of the area. Wibbly, Millie and the cats went to his side as they wanted to get involved.

"Send the password to Hopkin and Owain, Geraintus," instructed Molly as she started to think. The treasure chest needed to be opened, and she needed to keep her family alive along with access Castell Coch.

"Where's Hopkin then?" asked Bedivere suddenly as Geraintus was pebbling *"Kayealexaly,"* several times and back to front in case it was intercepted.

"Hopkin is the least of our worries," said Molly.

"We need the locket key of the spoon to open the drawbridge of this castle. Fabbles, Slobbers, I suggest you drop into Caroline Street and suss out all those people milling about. They're all harmless, enjoying a goblet of wine or two. Go and check, we need you to find the keyhole within the outskirts of the walls to open the drawbridge for us to fly in," instructed Gari looking at several dozen people wandering around near the castle entrance.

"Everyone is entitled to a goblet of wine or two, after all," said Ivor who fancied one himself but had to curb his need for the moment.

"That's probably all it is Gari," said Geraintus agreeing with Ivor and feeling a quench for some ale himself.

"Do you think it's occupied?" asked Wibbly.

"No, it's empty; but we need to secure it with our standard tonight before we leave in the morning," said Molly confident her next plan would work.

"The Ginger twins, you must stay here as Hopkin needs your locket. Fabbles, Slobbers, this is the map of the walled area. The keyhole is here," said Molly giving them a parchment that Hopkin had passed her a day or two ago in anticipation.

Double pins were inserted in the cats' fur as they were dropped from the coach in St. Mary's street on a corner where there was no one walking.

Quickly they scurried towards the twenty-foot walls of the castle and looked for the side wall, with steps that jutted out a little. They all watched anxiously in the coach as Molly sighed with relief. Her instructions had been accurate as they watched both cats climb over the wall swiftly and disappeared.

"Get ready to fly in, the drawbridge will soon come down," said Ivor excited for the first time that day.

***

"Can you see it?" asked Slobbers getting frustrated as he fought through the overgrown bushes near the entrance inside the grounds. No one had lived here for years it was apparent, but where was the keyhole?

"Here it is," shouted Fabbles who was now covered in some sticky plant and foliage. He looked like a commando as he beckoned with his paw to Slobbers where he thought was a keyhole.

Slobbers jumped over some shrub and made his way to Fabbles. If this gate opened it would be a miracle, he thought.

Indeed, it was a keyhole.

"Turn the key whilst I pebble the coach," said Slobbers quickly.

"Spell the grounds, Slobbers. We'll fly over the wall if you can't open the drawbridge. However, you must chant our spell before we can land with the treasures on board," instructed Molly from the coach.

"Why didn't we just do that?" thought Fabbles as he continued to try the key as Slobbers went to the middle of the overgrown lawn and chanted the Llewellyn chant.

"Huggle-Puggle; we're not trouble, no enemy; only ally; Kayalexaly, Kayealexaly," chanted Slobbers three times swishing his long tail in the air scattering angel dust given to him by Molly.

The coach responded and went into full throttle with Gari at the helm, as Bedivere hid under Geraintus believing they were going to crash. The coach flew over the wall and landed with a sudden jolt on a barren patch of ground directly in front of the castle entrance as Fabbles gave up trying the key.

Molly jumped out of the coach immediately and waved her tail at the lock, where Fabbles had failed. The drawbridge started to whine, and she immediately stopped it from opening, but satisfied they could open it, if needed.

"Good job Fabbles," she said. *"Wibbly, Millie, secure the castle and place our standard on the tower once you're happy it's empty. But best to double check,"* she instructed as Wibbly and Millie disappeared to fulfil their task.

Garibaldi confirmed inside the coach that everyone outside were celebrating a Welsh win at the rugby, and they'd arrived unnoticed. Bedivere, Geraintus stood next to Molly and Ivor outside the coach, feeling safe for the first time in a few days. They looked up in awe at the castle. This was the first one to be officially occupied by the Llewellyn family for an exceedingly long time.

Molly went to locate the servants; they were expecting them. Hopkin had seconded the kitchen staff and grounds staff a week earlier. Hopkin had anticipated all of this. He was remarkable, thought Molly as she went to introduce herself to her new kitchen and grounds staff.

Chapter 8

Hopkin Paulinus

"*I hope this pebble won't be long,*" thought Hopkin for the umpteenth time that morning. He'd had several days of the utmost trouble with these exasperating Eagles, and it was only a matter of time before he'd kill one of them. Or to the point one of them would kill him.

He'd had several flashbacks of happy memories as he'd glided towards the castle in his pink coach. Times he'd frolicked with his cousin Gilbert de Clare in the grounds of the castle, so long ago.

The castle was unusual as it was triangular and had rounded type curtain walls all around it. He remembered the trouble Gilbert had had when he built the connecting angled towers and marvelled at the sight in front of him. He'd forgotten how magnificent this castle was and how much love and care had gone in to creating it.

The drawbridge was open but Hopkin though it best not to fly in unexpectedly. He had instructed the coach to fly around the side of the wooded glades as not to frighten the eagles. The pink coach had descended onto the only blade of grass available to the side entrance to the cavern. The wooded glades surrounded three quarters of the castle presently and the landing was precarious indeed.

The Golden Eagles had been frightened by the arrival of a pink coach spewing pink smoke and dust that they'd attacked it brutally, cracking the unbreakable glass in several places. Hopkin hadn't been remotely prepared for this onslaught and had hidden inside the coach until he could remember the spell to calm the eagles down.

He had eventually remembered his hot poker spell, which always worked on any bird or animal that was having a temper tantrum. This described the Eagles perfectly and he set about spelling them to calm down,

"Lilir Ffagl/Leeleer fahgal," he repeated a dozen times waving his robes and cloak around him as he marched out of the coach looking far more confident than he'd felt. The Eagles immediately recognised his commanding voice and spell and stood in front of him, their deep-set golden eyes observing every move he made.

They chatted in Eagle language and Hopkin explained why he'd arrived and the purpose of his unexpected arrival prior to Magical Molly.

"I'm head of the Llewellyn family and have come to rescue you and the family from this dreadful occurrence," said Hopkin trying to be calm but he didn't feel calm at all.

"Prove it," screeched Eagle One.

"I'm Hopkin Paulinus, eldest brother before Ivor and Tudor. Ifor AP Meurig is our half-brother, and he is fighting with our cousins Owain Glyndwr and Gilbert de Clare. He left you, our most trusted warriors to protect the treasure chest until we found the missing treasures to link with it. This treasure belongs to the Llewellyn family, which is why I'm here. We need to prepare for Magical Molly's arrival with the found missing treasures, in order we can claim this Castle as rightfully ours."

"Is that THE Magical Molly?" enquired the Second Eagle who stepped towards Hopkin in earnest.

"Yes, she's on her way to secure the treasure and relinquish your work. She will rescue you and turn you back to faithful warriors once the chest has been opened," said Hopkin quietly hoping for a positive response.

"The grounds are free, you can enter the castle through the side door or drawbridge," said Eagle Two, *"But the treasure chest is in the tunnel, behind the cavern."*

"We need to prepare for Molly's arrival. I suggest you close the drawbridge, as she can enter the courtyard," suggested Hopkin as Eagle One nodded in agreement.

"We can't open the chest, we've tried everything," said Eagle Two. *"We desperately need to be free; we need a tiny key with a locket to open it."*

"Show me, we must hurry," said Hopkin. Something wasn't right and the sooner he found out to alert the others the better.

The treasure chest was in a tunnel and in front of the tunnel was the cavern full of dirty murky but silvery looking water. It fell to the wooded side of the castle and Hopkin realised it was a special cavern. No one could survive the water as it was spelled. He wondered how Molly had managed to live through it by falling in the well at Carew. She was obviously more magical and mystical than even he had imagined.

The treasure chest sat partially hidden by the clammy wall and was enormous. It was covered in a plethora of golden candles and half-moons, like the Golden Coracle. On seeing this for the first time, Hopkin became excited. The treasure chest held all the family parchments and personal information, and he wondered what secrets this family had over the years. He couldn't wait to find out.

The padlock on the chest was on its side and it had a link chain circling through it, the same as when Garibaldi reported to him, how they'd found the Golden Coracle. He wondered if the Croggs had anything to do with this, but they couldn't have. Ifor AP Meurig had secured this chest before going to war with Gilbert De Clare. However, he had another funny feeling and pebbled Gari at once.

"Stay in Cardiff until its safe. Send Gingers with the locket and key at once."

A different pebble arrived at his feet at the same time.

"Crogg army on way but so are we. Secure castle, have informed Molly."

"Eagles, we are being approached by the Croggs, secure castle right away. Are there any animals, mystical creatures, or enchanted persons nearby to assist?" asked Hopkin only glad the Eagles were at least on his side.

"No, we've safely sent everyone away, as that was our job," wailed Eagle two.

"Never mind, go Eagles, and prepare to attack from the tower. I'll repair my coach and send it back for the Ginger cats to return with the locket and key. We need to release you and the treasure as soon as we open the chest," instructed Hopkin quickly. *"I'll join you in a moment."*

"Marddanhadlen cochwyn Glas/Mahurdd-an-hadlane, koggueen glahce," he repeated several times showering a triple cuff of angel dust over the whole coach as it slowly repaired its own glass and took on armour of its own, a bit like double glazing. Hopkin went inside and set the controls to Cardiff. He spelled it to disappear the minute it hit the first silver cloud, which was on stand-by overhead.

It was important that the local farmers, working in the fields were not alerted to a floating foreign object. Tongwynlais was near to Cardiff Castle but far enough to create an army of nosey people in the middle of a potential fight. He'd sent a cloud formation earlier and he could only hope that Molly or Gari even had noticed his messages.

Hopkin watched as his pink coach purred out of view as it flew high towards the silver clouds which would escort it unseen and safely to Cardiff Castle.

***

"When are the Ginger's going?" asked Bedivere feeling much better knowing he was inside an unoccupied but secure castle.

"I'm sending them all," said Molly as Bedivere looked at her in aghast. They were all outside waiting for a clue from Hopkin and Molly had been watching the clouds for the past hour. Gari was re- setting the hovel and Geraintus had gone with Millie and Wibbly to clear the grounds and organise food.

Reuben, the new chief elf in the servants' quarters, were glad to accommodate their initial needs. They were overly excited that the Llewellyn family were going to reside in their Castle.

"Surely, we need them with us?" said Ivor.

As she mentioned this, Geraintus and the two dogs returned and all the cats regrouped from different areas, having had a brief with Garibaldi.

Bedivere went pale at the thought of Geraintus leaving him as Molly continued and realised, she needed to explain a few things whilst they waited for Hopkins' code.

"Geraintus, with your long strides and giant features, spy on Castell Coch, you'll be able to decipher how the battle with the Croggs are proceeding."

"Look," said Gari interrupting, *"the message from Hopkin, it worked."*

"Summon the cats Gari. They need to leave right away, the pink coach will land any minute," said Molly as Bedivere waited anxiously to find out what was going to happen to him.

The distant purring of the pink coach meant the cats had to be ready within minutes. Molly gave them all instructions and Gari was busy giving them all double pins and turquoise collars to enhance their magical attributes.

"Remember the chant, guys?"

"Huggle-Puggle, we're not trouble. Whispering fig tree is white. Golden Coracle mustn't have a fright. Wake up to Kayalexaly, Kayealexaly," they all said together.

*"Excellent, add **"wake up and open, Kayealexaly, Kayealexaly,"** at the end. Say it all three times, whilst you're massaging the chest to open. Ginger Two, you'll use your locket and key to open the padlock. You all deserve to do this together,"* beamed Molly.

They were all excited. Fabbles couldn't believe his luck. Three brothers and on a mission, he was over the moon. Slobbers looked at Molly and he knew she wanted him in control and swayed his tail in acknowledgment. He was still Top Cat, and he felt proud he'd three brothers equally committed to the cause. He must remember to tell Molly there was another brother missing but that would have to wait.

"They're ready," said Gari as Bedivere was getting agitated as everyone was leaving. Ivor held him back and whispered something in his ear. The pink coach clawed itself to a safe landing right next to the Three Feathers which twitched and recognised its counterpart.

"Pebble us, once the chest is open. We'll not be far behind," said Molly as they all scampered up the glass steps.

Wibbly Alf and Millie stood with respect for the cats and waved their tails with encouragement as the pink coach purred away straight into a silver cloud, hidden from the normal eye.

Ivor didn't want to leave and was worried about the Croggs.

"Are we going to fight the Croggs?"

"Bedivere, stay here and get this castle ship shape for when Geraintus returns," said Molly ignoring Ivor for a moment.

Bedivere looked visibly shocked as Molly smiled at him. *"You've been through enough. It's time you prepared this castle for you and Geraintus."*

Geraintus who had left the minute he'd been instructed hadn't explained anything to Bedivere at the time.

"Geraintus wanted me to inform you. He's going to live here with you, we're all going to share the animals and Gari will assist you in finding a servant to help. Once

Geraintus gives us an update on Castell Coch, he'll return to be with you."

"I thought Hopkin was going to live here, or you, Molly," said an incredibly pleased Bedivere and looked straight at a shocked Ivor.

"Hopkin will take Caernarvon Castle, now Tudor is no longer with us," said Molly.

Changing the subject but Ivor couldn't help but interrupt,

"Did you see that black cloud following the coach? You do realise they're being followed?" said Ivor amazed Gari and Molly seemed oblivious to this serious bit of observation.

***

Hopkin hoped they wouldn't be much longer. It should have been here by now, he thought to himself as he towered next to the Eagles in anticipation of the Croggs arrival to attack. He could see the odd one scurrying through the trees and hoped Owain's men wouldn't be too far away. He knew he had two Golden Eagles with a brutal and successful reputation for killing enemy, but the Croggs and bug dogs were a distinct species altogether.

He'd spent a considerable amount of time setting bomb clusters in the lawns and various surprise elements. He hoped his spells would work when the time came. He scoured the skies once again looking for the silver cloud, but nothing.

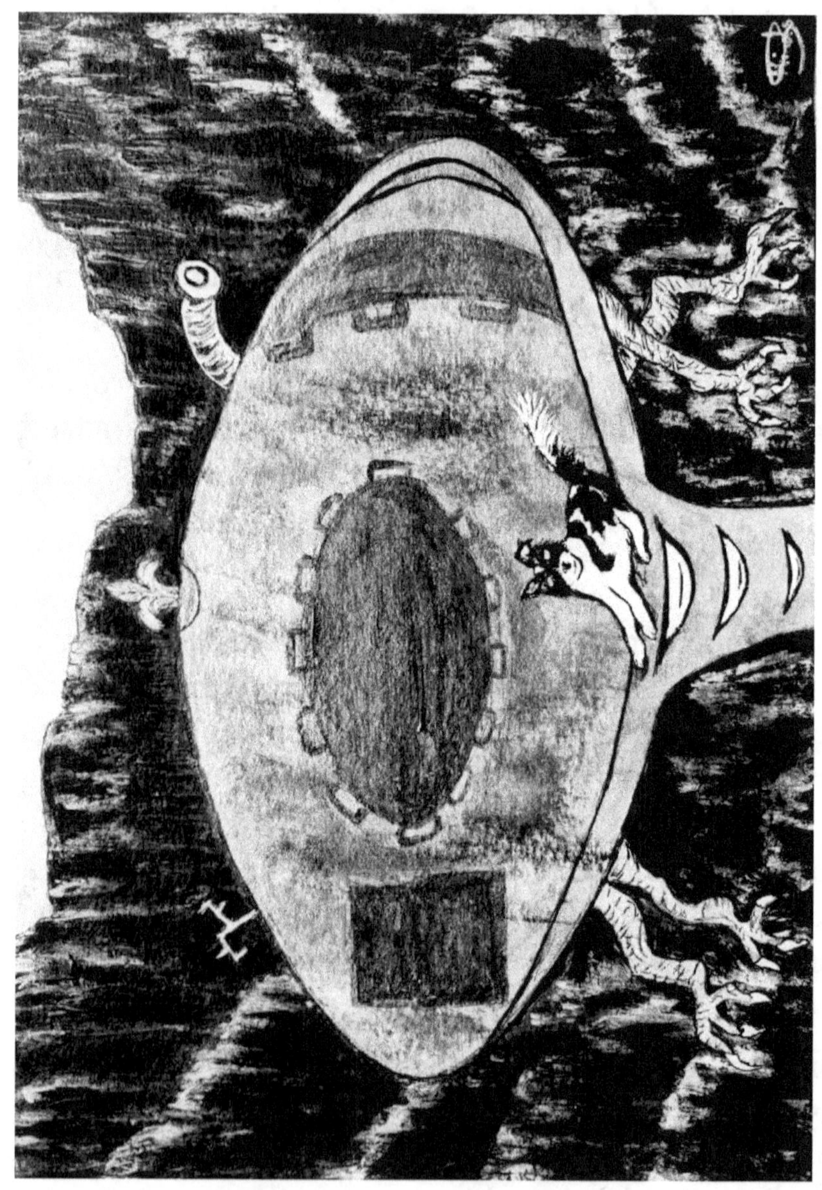

Oval coach descending at night

Chapter 9

Castell Coch

The pink coach was taking much longer to arrive than expected and Hopkin was losing patience. He kept seeing more Croggs scurrying through the trees towards the castle. His gut feeling told him something wasn't right, but he couldn't fathom what that was. He knew that Owain's army was about to arrive to support this next onslaught but then he saw it.

***

Kentav Crogg couldn't believe his luck. He'd stumbled across the codes for a secret cloud formation whilst they'd ransacked Ivor's cave, and he'd deciphered it perfectly. This incompetent family kept underestimating him. Indeed.

He was listening to the chatter of the Llewellyn's aboard one of their coaches. He hadn't gathered anything tangible, but he was convinced whoever was in that coach, was on their way to Castell Coch and would disclose information very soon. Someone was bound to say something in relation to the whereabouts of the spoon. He just had to be patient, they were bound to disclose where the coracle had been hidden too, he was sure of it.

***

Plonk, plonk. Plonk.

"Have they left yet?" said Gari reading aloud the pebble from Hopkin.

"They should be there by now," said Bedivere beginning to get alarmed.

"They're being followed by that black cloud," said Millie who'd been watching from the tower.

"Oh, my goodness," said Ivor, *"You know what that means Molly?"*

"Calm down Ivor," said Gari as he nodded for Wibbly and Millie to start patrolling the perimeter and guard the treasures within the coach.

"Of course I do, Ivor. That's why they've gone with a replica key and locket and not the original. They're quite safe Hopkin will tell the eagles about the cloud as soon as he sees it. The cats also know what to say on board and what not to say," smiled Molly completely in charge and Ivor felt foolish suddenly.

"The treasure chest won't open with a replica key Molly," said Bedivere quietly.

"Yes, it will," said Gari.

"Enough, we shall leave first thing regardless," said Molly. *"I suggest you concentrate on your new castle Bedivere and leave the final part of this treasure hunt to us."*

"Pebble Hopkin and inform him that the coach is slower as the eagles destroyed the glass. They should be in his sight very soon," said Molly.

Bedivere walked away in a huff as Garibaldi smiled at Molly and sent the crystal pebble in an instant.

***

Kentav Crogg hid under an oak tree and was totally dissatisfied with the coach party. He'd decided that Molly wasn't included in this trip but where was she? Slobbers, he'd deduced was inside and his lead Bug Dog had hated him, he was worth eliminating. He was losing his touch.

His wife Blodwen wasn't too happy with him either about his obsession with the Llewellyn treasure. Ali had been blown up before he'd defected to New Zealand and Trent had defected to the Llewellyn's in the name of love.

What had happened to Jethro and Bethesda he'd no idea He was losing his grip on his allies along with his business. At least he'd given Blodwen that envelope. He was going to take the castle once his men were in position and by any means. If he didn't get home with at least one treasure, his wife knew what to do with that envelope. However, he was more determined than ever to have Molly's head and to bring back to St. Clears the treasure that was rightfully his. He would be Lord of these castles, one way or another.

***

The black cloud was overhead and suddenly a pebble plopped inside the coach from Gari, warning them of the spy trap. Slobbers made tail signals, and the cats all responded and talked in even more riddles than earlier which made them all laugh even more.

Suddenly the coach veered to the right with a jolt which sent the cats into a bundle on the floor as the coach tilted from one side to another.

"Slobbers, what's going on?" wailed Fabbles forgetting for a moment they were being spied upon.

Slobbers looked through the looking spectacles on the dashboard and saw a great big eagle scooping towards them trying to break the cloud above.

He made further tail signals, as the cats all sat on the floor and held each other as the coach avoided the eagles as they tried to burst the cloud.

"They're going to crash land," thought Hopkin as he observed from inside the tower.

The coach suddenly assumed speed and careered towards the castle as it crashed into thousands of little pieces inside the courtyard. Hopkin ran so fast towards them that he fell over his cloak down the steps. He got up, shook himself for being so undignified and hoped as he entered the courtyard that they were at least alive.

Kentav Crogg, hiding in the woodland was mortified that they'd not landed on the lawn as he'd strategically placed bug dogs there ready to kill them. He became even more annoyed.

The cats were covered in shards of pink glass but otherwise unharmed. Hopkin sent a pebble immediately to Gari, to say all was well. He'd worry about the coach later. It needed a big fix but the treasure chest and fighting the Croggs was too important and imminent. He'd spotted Kentav Crogg and needed to start protecting the castle with the eagles before Owain arrived.

The arrows started to fly over the wall as the Croggs started to move forward. Suddenly there was an influx of armour. Hopkin waved his hand to Slobbers, to make their way to the cavern as he needed to protect the castle with the Eagles. Owain's men had arrived and Geraldus and Bevanuis appeared through the side door; to warn them, they were commencing battle.

Garibaldi and Molly watched on the hovel knowing that Kentav was still alive and relentless. He was after her and the treasure. It was imperative that they left together and soon. The battle had started and the Eagles and Owain's' men were far stronger than a hundred little Croggs. There was still an abundance of bug dogs, and it was important to kill them and eliminate Kentav, the last remaining Crogg.

"We're not going to wait," said Molly suddenly. *"I know the chest needs to be opened before we fly there with the two treasures, but we must go and assist Hopkin."*

"What do you need me to do?" asked Bedivere who realised, apart from the kitchen servants, he was going to be alone in the castle.

*"Prepare this castle for when Geraintus returns, he's on his way to you. Visit Eddlee Hornblov, the wise old wizard who resides at St. Mary's Street the tavern is called, "**The Wizard & Boar**." He's the proprietor and he'll provide you with a servant and suggest help. Gari will leave you the hovel and take you through spells that you may have forgotten. I'll get the coach ready with Wibbly and Millie."*

Wibbly Alf and Millie arrived in a second and the three dogs went to leave. The coach was opened, re-spelled and prepared for a swift journey and a sudden landing. Wibbly Alf was instructed to link up to the treasures and Millie started the controls.

Garibaldi left the hovel with Bedivere who looked more in control and felt important as he promised not to disappoint. He quickly realised that Gari had set the hovel, not only to track the family but also Geraintus' location. This reassured Bedivere right away as he waved the coach party over the wall.

Chapter 10

Eddlee Hornblov

"**S**ilence!"

The whole front room of the members only lounge in the "**Wizard & Boar**," public house fell silent. The dingy parlour sported a thick hume of cloud which lingered over the bar as the place was jammed packed full of Wizards of various seniority.

The elves were working at full capacity as the place was always packed, the first Monday of every moon calendar. This was the day, the Great Eddlee Hornblov gave suggestions and recommendations to Wizards, Elves, Gnomes, whoever needed his advice, without charging a fee or writing a notch in his black book, that he was owed.

As Eddlee had the honour of freedom of the City, he was able to get away with everything and sometimes he capitalized on this, for his own good. No one knew that Eddlee Hornblov was not as he appeared. He had fought the best and won but deep down he also had demons which on occasions clouded his vision but his loyalty to the First Family of Wales had never faltered.

Eddlee Hornblov had been Ivor Ap Llewellyn's key confidant for over a hundred years. Now and again, the wizards of the family would come along for a private audience and ask his advice or just receive some counselling of magical properties.

He knew everything about everyone as they would all confide in him. Eddlee Hornblov, however, kept transcripts of every meeting, unbeknown to his clients. What Eddlee didn't know wasn't worth knowing, he was instrumental in assisting everyone. Sometimes the price would be higher than the poor wizard, dwarf or elf could envisage.

Eddlee would use his knowledge and information later down the line to his own advantage and why not. He was the Greatest Wizard this side of the river Taff and had the freedom of the city to conduct himself in whichever manner he wanted. He was beyond reproach and kept his affairs close to his chest.

He was very aware of Ivor's capabilities and knew everything about him. He knew one day; this knowledge would become especially useful indeed. He knew all about Ivor's infidelities and the recipients and there had been a few. He was also aware of a few closed secrets regarding Ivor, which he knew that even Ivor himself didn't know yet.

Extortion wasn't Eddlee's idea of retribution, but he kept all this untold knowledge to himself until the time came for when he could use it, obviously for his own gain. In the meantime, as he listened to the wizard's chatter, he made a list who was present. Even though these consultations were free, there was no such thing as a free lunch. He knew that one day, these wizards would need him far more than he would need them.

He started the meeting as everyone had fallen silent.

"Right, everyone, who wants to start?"

"I'll go first if that's all-right folks, I need to return to my wife, she's in labour. Hope this is okay with everyone."

A room full of wizards nodded in agreement.

"I need to hand in this item. I'm not sure who it belongs to, but it's been moving around in our parlour. We think it must have attached itself to us whilst we were holidaying in North Wales. Is it possible to leave this with you and does anyone know if it has significant value to anyone, in order I can return it."

The young Wizard placed a misshaped hat on the counter. All the attendees craned to look at it and a murmur went round the room. Eddlee waved his hand for it to be passed throughout the room for everyone to have a look. He was sure he knew who the owner was but waited for everyone to have a look at it.

"Why is this significant Alfe," asked Eddlee.

"It keeps moving around as if its distressed or trying to tell me something, which obviously as it doesn't belong to me, I can't decipher what it's trying to do," Alfe explained.

"It's one of our wives, ladies in waiting hat as it's very colourful, especially with the red satin band on it.

What type of headwear is it, does anyone know? It does seems very animated."

Everyone watched the porkaht dance on the bar counter, it was red and white and supported a red satin band around the top of the brim. It looked as if it belonged to a discerning lady of substance. It was a very unusual size, and it looked as if it would only fit a lady's head.

"Let me have a closer look," asked Eddlee as it was passed along the wizards for him to examine it.

"It belongs to Garibaldi, Ivor's servant and dwarf," whispered Bedivere who did not wish to elaborate anymore, but he vaguely recognised it from years back.

"Really," said Eddlee as he examined it which made the pork pie hat even more agitated. *"Can you prove it, Bedivere."*

"I've seen it in Ivor's parlour, that's all I can say. I have no more information than that Eddlee. I can take it to him or ask him if you prefer."

"No no, there's no need, I can quantify you're right," said Eddlee not wishing to elaborate either as he'd seen inside the black lining of the red ribbon. Information, which he scanned very rapidly which might prove handy in the future. He handed it to Bedivere and asked him to return it to Garibaldi right away.

"Was there anything you needed Bedivere, while you're in the chair?" asked Eddlee making a few notes

in his head. He enjoyed and relished the gathering of information that could help him in the future.

"I'd like an audience with you to discuss Cardiff Castle. Once this open meeting has concluded," asked Bedivere being gracious as advised by Molly and Garibaldi.

"Granted, we'll talk after this meeting. Add Bedivere to the list," he ordered his elf who was scribbling furiously for him.

⚜

Chapter 11

Whispering fig tree

A large looming white shadow emerged over the Castle as Hopkin was briefing Bevanuis and Geraldus. The Eagles were squawking above, and the odd arrow was landing in the courtyard missing Hopkins' tall frame by inches. The men left the inner curtain to battle the Croggs, as Hopkin rushed to deal with the cats and help them de-shard their fur.

Plop, Plop, Plop.

The white shadow was coming nearer and Fabbles started to panic.

"What's that white thing coming towards the castle?" he asked as he picked some more glass out of his tummy.

"It's Geraintus he's marching this way. He'll be reporting back to the others. We must get you to the cavern at once. We need to open the chest," urged Hopkin darting from one foot to another as the arrows kept flying in from the front lawn. *"This is a pebble from Molly, she'll be here in twenty minutes we need to open the chest right away. Come follow me."*

***

Bedivere, having had a fruitful meeting with Eddlee Hornblov was also delighted to see Geraintus on the hovel. It wouldn't be long before he'd see him again.

***

The cats moved deftly and followed a nimble Hopkin Paulinus down the single path around the side of the castle as the path narrowed, the further along they went. The odd arrow kept missing them and the odd spark from the bug dogs, seemed to travel in the breeze, but so far so good. No one had been hit.

Hopkins' vibrant pink cloak flapped with urgency as the breeze picked up as they followed him with a sense of haste. Slobbers checked his collar and glanced behind him every so often as Fabbles checked too. The Ginger twins were close behind each other, both checking the lockets in their possession. One of the eagles flew overhead, which was reassuring as they arrived at the dark and dingy cavern.

***

"Can you remember the spell for the treasure?" asked Garibaldi who was sitting abreast of the communications dashboard and anxious as he'd lost touch with Slobbers. He'd been surprised that Molly had left the hovel with Bedivere. They'd no other form of staying connected with the cats and their progress. He felt incredibly nervous suddenly.

Both Wibbly and Millie looked surprised at this question and with one look from Molly, both realised that Gari was worried, because he'd no hovel as reassurance.

"*Yes,*" they both answered confidently.

Before Gari could challenge them, the Three Feathers coach made a clunking noise with Ivor reacting immediately.

"*What's that?*" he asked as Gari snapped out of his mood and went to investigate.

"*I've slowed the coach down,*" said Molly. "*We have a few things to discuss before we fly towards the castle.*"

Millie and Wibbly sat next to her as Gari and Ivor turned round from the dashboard to listen. Gari quickly forgot how he'd felt a minute earlier.

"*What's wrong?*" asked Ivor.

"*Ivor AP Meurig rescued a talented cat who was also very clever. She'd been abducted and she and her five kittens had been badly treated and spelled in several forms. They were dispersed throughout the kingdom before he could unleash the gift of spell, he'd given one of the kittens.*

Ifor AP Meurig had no choice, he wasn't sure if any kitten had been given a hypnotic spell to infiltrate or safeguard even, the family papers. With that in mind he decided to transform the best two men he had to look after and protect his treasure, our treasure as the security he endured was under threat.

He knew that the security of the family's heritage and future was under threat. Therefore, he transformed the Knights into Golden Eagles to protect what is rightfully ours. This treasure chest, however, can only be opened by one of his cats. Four of the five cats are in the cavern now, opening the chest. We need to give them a bit of time. That's why I've sent them together Gari. They're after all more family than you or me," said Molly as Gari nearly busted with pride as it dawned on him that Slobbers was indeed the most important cat in the land.

"When did you know all of this?" asked Ivor in awe of Molly yet again. He hadn't told her anything, he should have, but he'd forgotten until now. He knew that sooner rather than later he would have to tell her other things, but he couldn't bring himself, he was too ashamed. *"There were five cats altogether and they were not treated that well by the owner or by the supervising owner, if I recall. It was many moons ago. Ifor Ap Meurig rescued them and in turn, the cats rescued me.*

"It doesn't matter when I've known Ivor. It's important to tell them once they've achieved their task. Gari you can tell them once this is over. There's one brother missing. They can source their other brother once our treasure hunt's complete," said Molly making Ivor feel better. *"We need to land inside the castle and meet Geraintus, he's ready to plant the tree and hope that the cats have opened the chest by this time. Then we'll have all our faculties much stronger than ever to fight, any remaining Croggs and bug dogs."*

The coach purred slower than ever and Gari visibly relaxed. Wibbly and Millie were overwhelmed by Molly's magical and mystical knowledge and knew they were in safe hands. Ivor began to realise that he needed to tell Molly more family matters as by the sounds of things, she would soon find out, regardless.

He wondered if she knew all his deep dark secrets already. She couldn't know, otherwise she would have insisted he tell everyone. He sighed; he was dreading the time that he would have to spill the beans. He knew they would all be disappointed in him.

*****

Bevanuis and Geraldus had planned a strategy with Owain Glyndwr. After talking with Hopkin, they went through the rear of the castle and formed their plan. They had over a hundred hooded horses and men along with a hundred-foot soldiers.

Owain had realised he'd caused the family more grief than assistance and had been responsible for killing their flying hen, Gertrude. This was his way of making amends. The horses had been given plaques on their legs to protect them along with extra jacquard blankets under the saddles covering their bellies. Their eye protectors had been strengthened as they were aware of the killing sparks of the Beggly army.

The foot soldiers were also adorned with longer protective armour and were carrying spears and arrows. They wore colourful robes and metal headwear for extra protection. This would slow them down but protection against the antennae sparks was paramount. They covered the side of the castle and moved forward in a line; the horses all trotted steadily. The foot soldiers were situated in-between each horse ready to throw their spears and attack the Croggs. Some of the troops had moved to the other side of the lawns and had started to attack the Begglys.

Kentav Crogg had a catastrophic fit, when he realised how many horses and soldiers, the Llewellyn's suddenly had on their grounds. He waved his arm in the air and summoned the Croggs to move forward as the Begglys scurried through the men ready to attack, antennae's swirling round in anticipation and waiting for Kentav's order.

The Croggs had come prepared; their tall hats had been replaced by helmets to protect their bald heads. Tabards with reinforced wooden straps were worn over their costumes. They carried a long pouch on their backs made of sacking which held several pointed spears that had been made in the factory in haste. The ends were sharp and a few of the Crogg members had holes in their thumbs to prove it. The women in the factory had also been busy and had double knitted knee pads for their men, which would help them move about faster and protect them from arrows from the soldiers. They also looked taller which was a result of their boots having extra soles fitted. This was to help them square up to the soldiers as their height was always at a disadvantage. Kentav hoped that the Begglys would see to the enemy before they had to worry about close contact.

However, when Kentav saw the strength of the enemy, he was even more determined to find the treasure.

"Molly and the treasure must be here," he thought to himself. *"Why would the whole army come out in force just to protect this small castle?"*

He waved his arm in the air giving the Croggs and Begglys the go ahead to attack. They came from every crevice of the bushes and forest as the Begglys crawled towards Owain's horses, the men waiting for them and the Crogg army to get closer.

Bevanuis and Geraldus with separate troops started to throw their spears to off foot the Croggs. The men on horseback, held large shields which started to work as the antennae sparks from the Begglys began to bounce back, hitting the original Beggly in the back, killing them.

Kentav panicked and let them continue as he scurried away from the battle, this was going to be annihilation, but he had other plans. He knew he was a coward, but he also knew where the treasure was hidden. He disappeared from Geraldus' view and the Crogg troops started throwing their spears over the castle wall as well as at the horses.

***

Owain's men were beginning to make inroads on the lawn and the surrounding woodland as Geraintus' heavy frame came closer. His shadow was as enormous as the giant whispering fig tree.

Geraintus huffed and he puffed and made larger strides than normal as he walked towards the castle. The tree was very agitated as Geraintus clung to its roots knowing it could root anywhere it wanted. It hadn't been too happy to be moved and Geraintus had promised a surprise for it which had kept the tree from being a nuisance whilst in transit. The tree had been uprooted so many times in the past with false promises of finding the treasure, it simply had had enough. Knowing Magical Molly was going to be its new master had sufficiently calmed the tree enough to be carried at great pace without a stop.

He was close now and decided to walk towards the side of the castle avoiding the battle that was intense on the lawn. He observed Welsh hats being thrown in the air as Croggs fell and he could see sparks flying as the remaining bug dogs were fighting to save themselves along with their leader. He couldn't see Kentav Crogg, but he didn't look that closely. His mission was to plant the tree as quickly as possible and wait for Molly's arrival.

***

The three feathers coach came into view of the castle, but inside the silver cloud. Ivor scoured the lawn for Kentav Crogg as did Gari and Molly swished her tail over everyone, making them more magical as they entered the battle zone. The coach would soon land inside the courtyard and Hopkin needed to know,

"Gari send Hopkin a pebble. We'll be over to help once we've spelled the tree to the ground."

"Yes, good thinking," said Gari and he then realised he had a castle to organise.

"We need to keep Molly within sight at all times Wibbly," instructed Ivor. *"Kentav Crogg doesn't know what he's doing. All he wants is Molly's head, unless he stumbles on our treasure."*

"We need to protect this treasure, they're all in one place now," said Gari thinking this was even more of a worry especially as they hadn't spotted Kentav Crogg fighting. *He's dead already,* he hoped.

"Wibbly, Millie, once we get inside the castle, I suggest you stay with the treasures within the coach until we know Kentav is dead, and the treasures are ready to be married together," suggested Molly. She was also aware that this was even riskier to bring the treasures to the castle, knowing Kentav was eager to capture her along with the treasure. If he'd any idea that the treasures were in this coach, they would be in trouble.

Gari manoeuvred the coach silently inside the courtyard as the Eagles soared overhead. They recognised the coach and ignored it as the arrows were flying towards them with great gusto. In between assisting the army to kill the Begglys they took it in turns to fly over the cavern area to protect the cats as they continued their attempt to open the treasure chest. It was proving harder than any of them had envisaged.

"At no cost leave this coach," instructed Molly. *"We'll go and seal the whispering fig tree to position and then help the cats. Ivor, Gari, you come with me and then you'll need to prepare the castle."*

"What about your protection?"

"Geraintus will be free before he goes to Cardiff castle."

"Let's go, we're wasting time," said Gari anxious to get the tasks done.

"What if we see Kentav Crogg?" asked Millie.

"Kill him," said Molly, Gari and Ivor together as they left Wibbly and Millie in no doubt what to do.

Wibbly and Millie stayed inside the coach, locked themselves in and attached each other to the treasures. This way, they knew they were safe and spelled.

***

Geraintus huffed and puffed his big frame through the orchard, and he was there. It was soon time to plant the tree, and he knew Molly was on her way.

Eagle One had spotted Geraintus at the east side of the castle and on schedule. He dropped a pebble at Gari's big feet as they were making their way to meet him.

"Geraintus is here," he whispered as they moved quickly towards him. The quicker they secured the tree, the quicker the bird communication would kick in and the easier it would become to track the enemy in

general. This was an important part of the Llewellyn's schedule in keeping abreast of community goings on.

The tree was still white, and the cats needed to open the chest before it turned green. Geraintus wasn't sure if anyone else was aware. The treasure chest was a powerful safe and it was going to take the cats' more than one attempt to open it.

He only hoped Molly knew the spell to open it sooner rather than later. The cats, according to the historic paperwork had to attempt to open the chest primarily.

Geraintus stood behind the barn as Gari, Molly and Ivor arrived.

"Good Geraintus, let's plant her right away," said Gari.

"Whispering fig tree, whispering fig tree, you truly understand. White becomes green. Where the family stands. Kayealexaly, Kayealexaly, Kayealexaly," chanted Geraintus using his hands as shovels to cover the tree root system in the rich soil of Castell Coch.

Molly swished her tail and repeated the chant again scattering angel dust over all the branches as the tree shuddered in recognition of its new home. Ivor and Gari shook hands with the lower branches, and they swayed and acknowledged the Wizard and Dwarf as its new master. It sighed heavily and stopped swaying.

"She's ready to sleep we'll come and check it first thing. She'll have turned green by the morning, unless we've trouble opening that chest," said Geraintus.

"Come on, we need to see the cats," said Molly knowing that the chest was giving them grief. Nothing had been easy since her arrival. She guessed this last treasure had more than one secret embellished inside. The chest wasn't going to open for anyone without the right treasures. They had the treasure, but they needed to confirm its content.

Molly ran back to the coach followed closely by Gari and Ivor. Geraintus striding behind them knowing time was of the essence.

Wibbly and Millie were locked inside, and Molly waved her tail asking them to stay inside.

"Geraintus find Kentav and get a status report, I'm going to follow the path to the tunnel," said Molly.

Ivor looked at Garibaldi and they decided the same as they'd plenty of time to sort the castle. Right now, the chest needed everyone's input, and they nodded at Geraintus who went to search for Kentav Crogg.

"No Ivor, Gari, you stay here. Secure the courtyard, repair the pink coach, and keep an eye on the treasures, you've done enough," said Molly as she disappeared.

***

Kentav Crogg had been very clever and was feeling incredibly pleased with himself. He'd managed to find his way through the undergrowth and forestry to the side of the castle. One of his bug dogs was with him, they were dwindling fast in numbers, but he'd realised that they'd no chance of winning against Owain's army. He was determined to find someone for a ransom or find the spoon. The family were here or coming here and something was happening, and he was single-minded enough to find out what that was.

Before coming to attack, he'd had inside information from an old gardener, who'd worked in the castle several years previously. This gentleman was able to give him precise detailed instructions of the layout of the castle and the hidden ravine that he was trying to locate. He had been tipped off that there was something significant hidden in the ravine that no one until now, had access. He knew about the Eagles which made him feel even more confident that he was on to something.

He'd disposed of his tall Welsh hat as that would have made him conspicuous. He hadn't bothered with one of the new armoured caps his factory had made. He had no intention of getting killed, he had other ideas. He'd made good ground with the bug dog furrowing in front of him, making his crawl through the undergrowth that much easier. The hedges and bushes were very prickly indeed and Kentav was glad suddenly that he was only four foot and not six.

The whole area was on a long steep slope and the bush and forest stopped at the cavern edge where Hopkin was positioned outside it. To Hopkin's right was the very narrow path that they'd all walked from the inner courtyard and was only one foot in width. He was only a few feet away from the clearing near the cavern when he heard a shriek. It made Kentav jump, and he crouched even further into the bush as the eagle might have spotted him, but he wasn't sure.

Golden treasure chest in cavern

Chapter 12

The treasure chest

"Careful where you walk," said Hopkin as they had arrived at the entrance of the cavern as the eagles were flapping their large wings overhead.

The cavern was an eerie place, and they entered in single file. It was dark and Slobbers immediately waved his paw over the rugged slate wall and an instant light shone so they could see a bit better.

Fabbles stood in awe as he looked at the dark slick of water in the cavern, which covered three quarters of the area. Ginger One and Two stood with him as they realised this was the dangerous water that Hopkin had mentioned earlier.

They also knew that Molly had survived her time in the water and had returned safe to the cave at Saundersfoot. However, this didn't mean they were infallible. Not one of them thought for one moment they could survive this black and silver slimy water which looked like an oil slick...

As the cats were in awe of the water, Hopkin was studying the treasure chest, which was in the corner of the cavern, and it was much grander than he'd remembered. Slobbers, at his side was thinking the same thing and beckoned the others to look at the carvings. The gold crest of the golden cup along with candles and moons covered the chest even the sides. Although there was only a dim light from what Slobbers had produced, the treasure chest shone through the old cavern which made dancing shadows on the sloping cave roof and created an eerie but magical spell over everyone.

The Eagles shrieked outside the entrance bringing them back to the present as even Hopkin had momentarily been hypnotised by the magnificence of the chest. The shrieking continued as Slobbers and Fabbles went outside to investigate. Hopkin summoned the Gingers over as the chest needed to be opened right away.

Slobbers and Fabbles went scurrying down the sharp narrow path which was on a slope to see what the commotion was about. The eagle was swooping down in front of them and then they saw it. Slobbers froze on the path as Fabbles bumped into him,

"What is it bruv?"

"The eagles' are avoiding the sparks from that bug dog; look, it's infiltrated the side of the castle and trying to attack the eagle with those antennae I told you about. We need to kill it."

"How?" whispered Fabbles, as he hid behind Slobbers as they'd both gone to the side of the path to hide behind a laurel bush.

"Let's lure him into the cave and drown him in that murky water, they can't swim," said Slobbers.

"Why don't we just get that eagle to kill it?"

"No, we mustn't leave any trace just in case there are any more wandering around or Kentav Crogg even. The less evidence on the path the better."

Fabbles waved his tail at the eagle that nodded and flew towards them, luring the bug dog to follow as its antennae threw off sparks every two seconds. Eagle One flew up and down to avoid them and suddenly the bug dog saw Slobbers. Ah yes, he recognised this was the Fat cat, the camp had been discussing, and he was on their hit list.

He was programmed to kill anything that had registered on his spark system and Slobbers was one of them. It immediately got on the path and started to swirl its revolving legs mechanically towards the cats. It started to throw intense sparks at them as Fabbles scampered ahead, to warn the others. Slobbers moved swiftly and far enough away to avoid the sparks hitting him.

Slobbers entered the cave and Fabbles was waiting. As soon as the bug dog ventured inside, the two cats thumped him with their tails which sent it rolling and tumbling into the silvery murky water never to be seen again. The splash covered both cats, but their thick fur protected them.

Slobbers and Fabbles looked pleased with themselves as the Eagle continued to flap its wings as he continued to swoop overhead to protect the cavern.

Hopkin was exasperated in the corner of the cavern as the two Gingers had not yet succeeded to open the chest and help was required immediately.

"Come on you two, the Gingers need some help. I'm going to re-spell the cave. You two need to massage those symbols, this heavy link chain, and chant the riddle as Ginger's locket isn't working yet," commanded Hopkin more exasperated than annoyed.

"Dewinynyrogof, anifeiliadynbrysusasaf"/ dehweenuhnuhogov, ahneevealeeadh-uhn bryseerah-saaff," as he repeated the complicated but sensitive spell three times and swished his pink cloak all over the cavern scattering even more angel dust over everyone.

However, the cats continued to chant, as Ginger was prising the key and locket in the eyelet hole patiently and every three seconds, but to date nothing.

"Molly's here," said Hopkin quietly as a pebble arrived while he patiently watched.

The chanting got louder with this news and the cats continued to work every inch of the chest.

***

Molly was pacing up and down inside the inner courtyard. Something was bothering her, and she couldn't put her paw on it. She's sent Wibbly Alf and Millie to check on Geraintus who'd been asked for a battle status, regarding Kentav Crogg but he hadn't returned. She needed to help the cats but had a feeling regarding Kentav Crogg. She knew she was being hunted and even though she could easily finish him off, she was more inclined to reserve her powers for the next task.

Wibbly and Millie returned and rushed through the back gate out of breath as Geraintus followed them. She'd sent Gari and Ivor to sort the castle in readiness as she'd stood outside the coach, guarding the two treasures, until Wibbly and Mille returned. Wibbly was anxious to tell her,

"We've no idea on the whereabouts of Kentav Crogg. He's not been killed, and he's not retreated and there are still around fifty men battling out on the lawns. There are around twenty bug dogs but even some of them are returning home. Kentav Crogg is missing."

"What do you mean Kentav Crogg is missing?" asked Ivor as he'd come out to investigate the noise that Wibbly and Millie had made through the back entrance. Geraintus was greener than usual, and Molly had to compose herself.

"Stop worrying Ivor. I suggest you lock yourself in the castle. Wibbly and Millie along with Geraintus can secure the coach and treasures. I'll go and help the cats in the cavern and between us we'll find Kentav. He can't be far away. He's after me, and if I leave the courtyard at least it should avoid him from coming in here. The last thing we need is the treasures to be discovered. You must kill him if you see him don't hesitate. Go Ivor. On no account leave the coach and treasures," said Molly

as she swished her tail in the air and departed through the courtyard towards the path.

Ivor and Garibaldi started to secure the courtyard and Wibbly and Millie linked themselves to the treasures again. Geraintus stood guard outside the coach, they'd got it covered.

Molly was ahead on the path and couldn't help but feel that something wasn't right. They'd all arrived here safely, Owain had fought their battle for them, and she hadn't done a thing really but got them all here. She walked very deliberately and carefully on the narrow path knowing it was going to get narrower. She could see the eagles soaring ahead and she knew she was getting close. She was pleased that the cats had found each other, and she couldn't wait to tell them more about their Guardian and where they had lived. She looked up and froze.

Kentav Crogg was on the path, in front of her but facing the cavern ahead. His clothes were torn, and his legs were bloodied obviously from creeping around in the bushes. She moved silently behind a prickly bush next to the path to compose herself. She craned her neck to look even further down the path and there was a bug dog rolling in front of Kentav, very slowly in one of those moss jackets they'd discovered earlier round the beach head.

Hopkin looked as if he was daydreaming as he was stood outside the entrance of the cavern distracted and not looking her way. He wanted to be the first wizard in the chest; he knew there was something important in there, that Kentav Crogg wanted. There was no way he was going to allow anyone to read the parchments before he had sight of them.

"I need to eliminate him right now," she thought to herself as a pebble dropped at her feet. She opened it and it was a warning pebble from Gari saying Kentav was missing.

"He's right here," she thought as she prepared herself to kill him. It was time. She pebbled Hopkin and the eagles, warned Ivor, to protect the inner courtyard as she was about to blow up Kentav Crogg.

She prepared herself and crept up behind Kentav, her tail tall and erect in the air as she swished her tail three times........

Hopkin had spotted Kentav and the bug dog as he looked out of the cavern. The eagles had disappeared, and he decided to take matters in his own hands. He needed to see inside this chest. He would kill Kentav himself.

"Hopkin look," cried Slobbers excited from deep inside the cavern. *"The chest is opening, Hopkin the chest.... Look."*

Hopkin mumbled an apology to the cats as the creaking sound of the treasure chest echoed throughout the cavern. He needed to take control at once.

He swished his triple cloaked cuff over the cavern and commanded,

"Hocus crocus, daffodils too; forgive me the rest is taboo."

He flung his cloak in the air along with both hands and a crack of lightning hit the air outside.

"Diweddybachgen, Lladdarunwaith/Deewadth-uh-bahggdden, llahdd-ah-eenwaheeth," as Molly threw her tail in the air spun three times at precisely the same time as Hopkin.

The second bug dog, who couldn't fathom where his mate had disappeared to, but saw Hopkin sent a triple set of sparks from his antennae as Kentav turned around as he heard the first crack.

All three spells collided with brute force and got flung in the air as the first crack hit the cavern full on both inside and out. The noise reverberated round the cavern area and Castle grounds.

Ivor and Garibaldi had run for cover inside the castle and Geraintus was inside the coach with Wibbly and Mille expecting the worst.

A split second later the second two sparks set off the spell from Molly and bounced off the crack causing spell mayhem and chaos. Neither spell could decipher their instructions, and the resulting catastrophic explosion could be heard for miles around the community.

The sky turned black, and the thunder responded to the lightning strike as the ground trembled in fear. The wind turned up as a hurricane of tornedo proportions. This completely wrong-footed Molly and threw her down the slope at a hundred miles an hour ploughing through bushes and prickly hedges in her path.

Inside the cavern was sporting thick black smoke as it over spilled outside as Hopkin laid in a heap, at the front entrance. His pink cloak was as black as soot and burning in patches. The Eagles returned to see if they could get near the cavern, but it was impossible to see inside, let alone get close. They observed Hopkin in a black heap at the entrance. They soared away to tell Garibaldi.

Geraintus had steadied the coaches and had run immediately he heard the first crack. Ivor and Garibaldi shortly followed as Wibbly and Millie looked on. They both wanted to go and rescue and realised how Yo-Yo had felt guarding the treasures and yet they wanted to be useful.

"I'll stay here," said Wibbly, *"I know you need to go."*

Millie licked his big face with appreciation and scurried after the wizards, hoping that Hopkin, the cats, and Molly had survived the blast. The loudest blast anyone had heard in an exceedingly long time.

Chapter 13

The aftermath

Molly had been dragged for over a hundred feet through bushes and prickly hedges towards the whirlpool of smouldering water. This was part of the caverns' water system at the edge of the forest. She came to a stop peacefully unaware of the calamity inside the cavern.

Hopkin eventually stirred and patted himself all over to check he was intact as he slowly got up. The thick black smoke had subsided, as he spelled his smouldering cloak to revert back to its normal pink flamboyant state. Ivor, and Garibaldi along with Geraintus arrived out of breath. The eagles both soared overhead.

"Where's Molly," shouted Ivor over the strong wind which had responded to the onslaught. Gari rushed past them and went inside the cavern as the black smoke had subsided. He started to wail as loud as the eagles as both Ivor and Hopkin rushed inside after him.

Gari was trying to reach over the curdling water as a dead cat floated on it. Ivor reached and brought it closer as Gari started to wail again as he pulled Fabbles from the murky water.

"Where are the others?" he screamed as they all tried to get a focus on the inside. The Ginger twins were splattered on the ground, paws missing and tails.

"Where's Slobbers?" whispered Gari as he stared at the chest as did Ivor. Slobbers was stuck to the opened lid and had taken the full blast on his back. His body was in several pieces as Gari started to howl like a wolf and held his remains to him in hysteria. He sat on the damp ground cradling pieces of his beloved cat as Ivor and Hopkin; both stunned started to look for Molly.

"She was on the path Ivor."

Millie arrived with Geraintus who had gathered evidence from the path on their way to the cavern.

"Kentav Crogg is in bits and a bug dog, all his body parts, what we can actually recognise is in this basket." His orange tuft of hair was in Geraintus' hand to prove he'd been killed.

"Oh no," shrieked Millie as she realised what had happened inside the cave as Gari continued to wail. His fat tears rolled down his cheeks, he was shaking and inconsolable.

"Millie, search the area for Molly, hurry. Take an Eagle with you," said Ivor.

The eagles were questioning already why they hadn't been transformed into warriors and had started to get agitated. Molly was the only magical dog that could administer the spell; therefore, it was imperative to locate her. They didn't need telling twice as they flew overhead to assist Millie in their search.

Ivor looked at Hopkin and then the open chest. He desperately wanted to look inside. He couldn't remember if some or all of his past secrets were logged in there. He knew he'd have to confess earlier than he wanted to, as he was sure Hopkin was also curious. However, it had to wait.

"Ivor take Gari and the cats back to the inner courtyard we can bury them in the morning. What do you think?"

Ivor sighed as he was fighting back tears of his own. He couldn't console his best friend and servant, and he didn't want to leave as Molly was missing. He wearily got up from the damp ground and reluctantly agreed. He knew Hopkin was going to rummage through the chest before him, but at that moment he didn't care. Whatever was in the chest, he would have to explain himself at some point. He was too tired to bother, he was consumed by Gari's and his loss.

"The eagles and Millie are looking for her Ivor. Well timed Geraintus," said Hopkin as the green giant had gathered all the evidence outside. He had also spelled a casket from Wibbly to house the remains of the cats. The mere sight of the casket had resulted in Gari having another bout of wailing. He was rocking back and forth, his beloved Slobbers held tight on his bloodied chest. Flabbers' body was on his lap, he was covered in their blood and became hysterical once more.

Hopkin and Geraintus laid all the remains in the casket and Hopkin waved his hand and a silk cloak appeared. They scoured the wet cavern floor and retrieved the four lockets with the keys amazingly attached and intact. Ivor gently prized the remains of Slobbers and Flabbers from a heartbroken Gari, and they covered the casket with the cloak. *"At least our spells are working,"* thought Hopkin.

"Geraintus take the casket and take Ivor with Gari to the courtyard. I'll go and help Millie. Send Wibbly Alf to assist us," said Hopkin quietly.

Millie had started searching beyond the path after she'd realised that Kentav's remains were in the same vicinity. She'd been told of the hurricane force wind and had started to move away from the area in her search. She was comforted to know that an Eagle was overhead. He'd instructed the whispering fig tree of developments and if any birds in the kingdom were flying overhead and saw her, they'd be notified immediately.

She looked up as Eagle Two was shrieking and then she saw her mate running towards her, albeit carefully due to the havoc the blast had created. Wibbly Alf caught up and she told him about the cats. They embraced and together they started to search down the steep slope.

Hopkin couldn't help it; he knew it was distasteful, but he had to look through the treasure chest before anyone else. Now was his chance as the dogs were looking for Molly. He hoped the blast hadn't destroyed the parchment they needed to confirm the treasure was theirs. They knew this already but there was much needed and missing Llewellyn paperwork, which would eliminate any other idiot, like Kentav Crogg to challenge the treasures in the future.

The treasure chest was full of old and worn-out looking papers. Hopkin rummaged through carefully, not wishing to damage any papers regardless of what they may contain. He found various chattels and documents referring to the family history. There was a turquoise stone in a silver and purple/bluish pouch and enough gold bouillons to keep the family secure for decades.

There were two feathered covered unique purses embellished with pearls and stones, which looked regal and interesting. Towards the very bottom and well-hidden were several thick brown fragile looking files that had seen better days. Hopkin's heart beat a bit faster as he gently removed them from the chattels and mementos.

As he opened the first file, a loud shriek came from the outside as he hurried to see.

"It's Molly, we've found her we need help," shouted the eagle as Hopkin placed all the files safely in a concealed pocket of his long flamboyant cloak and hurried after Eagle One.

Millie and Wibbly had no idea what to do next, hence they'd asked the eagle to fetch Hopkin. She was in

Flamboyant Hopkin Paulinus

a poor state and Millie couldn't feel a pulse. Eagle Two sat next to her. She was burned; her tail was missing and Wibbly had gone to locate it. Her paws were scorched, and one was hanging from her leg, her body was burnt severely in patches, and she was rigid. Millie was soothing her tummy with her paw and willing her to breathe or even wake up. One ear was torn away, and she was bleeding profusely.

Wibbly returned with a tail and attached it to her, with the aid of some spearmint he'd found within the bushes. *"That might help it knit until we get her back to the castle."*

As he said this, Hopkin arrived with Eagle one overhead.

"We need a stretcher of some kind straight away Hopkin to carry her to the castle."

Hopkin tried to find a pulse and failed but looked at Millie then Wibbly. *"We'll save her,"* he said quietly.

"Ffwlbri, Ffwlbri/foolbree," Hopkin waved his hand, and a few silver cloaks appeared. *"Atom Tempo, atom tempo,"* as two poles appeared.

Very deftly Hopkin prepared a stretcher, and the two Eagles were now flapping their wings intensely overhead waiting for their task.

"We need to move her slowly but let me try and stop the bleeding. "Sagra, Sagra.""

The bleeding appeared to stop. Wibbly and Millie with Hopkin carefully moved her slowly over the cloak which started to gather around her the minute she was centre to the poles. The Eagles flew downwards and with both their beaks on each side, they balanced and carried the stretcher and flew slowly towards the inner courtyard. Hopkin, Wibbly and Millie walked up the slope following the stretcher with Hopkin using the poles to keep his balance until they reached the cavern.

"We need to bring the treasure chest Wibbly. Can you and Millie carry it between you, I need to light a green candle and start a soothing spell on Molly right away. Inside the chest is a turquoise stone. Quick find it, I've just realised why it's in there," instructed Hopkin as a green candle appeared from nowhere and the senior family wizard started to chant.

Wibbly found the stone and the Eagles flew lower. Hopkin turned the collar of an unconscious Molly, and the turquoise stone grasped its space immediately within the collar. Wibbly and Millie looked at each other amazed as they continued in single file, sometime sideways through the narrow path towards the castle courtyard.

Geraintus was as shocked as everyone, but the whispering fig tree had turned green, which meant it was now fully functional. Gari was still sobbing over the casket and Ivor wasn't much help. Geraintus knew that Hopkin wouldn't be too pleased not to find the Castle ship shape, especially as they needed a room to heal Molly. He'd had enough.

"Ivor, Gari. Molly is on her way back; she's in a bad way. The only way she's going to heal if we're ready for her. Gari, she'd expect you to be making Welsh cakes and spring cleaning the place. Ivor, she'd have expected you to have all her trunks and yours unpacked by now. Come on, we've been told by Owain there are no threats outside we've truly won. We've no excuses. You're only letting Molly down, if you fail to get her quarters tidy before Hopkin arrives with her on his stretcher. Go right away. I'm staying here to guard the treasures," commanded Geraintus as green as the Welsh hills and angrier than he'd ever been seen to be by Ivor in his entire life. Gari was shocked to hear his tone too and left Slobbers in the casket and scurried after Ivor, they had work to do.

Chapter 14

The Llewellyn family

A pebble plopped at Geraintus' feet as he was handing out orders. He picked it up and a smile appeared on his giant face as he read the encouraging message from Bedivere. He looked forward to living with Bedivere too and he felt comforted that Bedivere was keeping a watchful eye on the hovel and his welfare. That made him more determined to organise everyone in order he could leave and join him at Cardiff Castle.

As he was pondering this and writing a pebble to Bedivere the treasures inside the coach started to twitch as Geraintus hurriedly threw the pebble in the air slightly alarmed at this noise. Ivor and Garibaldi, who'd taken on Geraintus orders to the letter, rushed out as they heard the melodious music.

Gari tripped and fell over the cloaks he was carrying as Ivor stood still. Geraintus had fixed the pink coach whilst he'd been guarding the treasures and apart from the odd uneven join, it was near perfect.

"Why, you've done a good job," said Ivor.

"We need to move the treasures," said Gari re-arranging the cloaks in his arms. *"The treasure needs*

to be united with that chest when it comes. It's better to have them all inside, it will be more secure."

"We need the green candle that's inside the treasure chest to place it on the ash seat," said Ivor astounding Geraintus as he hadn't mentioned this before. *"I also need to investigate what's in it, as soon as they get here."*

Gari looked on in disgust at his master. Ivor had not given any information to anyone during this horrendous fight to keep the treasure and he was unhappy with him. He silently blamed Ivor for everything. He should have a little chat with Molly.

"Let me show you," said Ivor already his powers returning.

Inside the coach the coracle was indeed agitated and was rocking back and forth, the Hugglett spoon attached to its link chain glowed as if in agreement. On the ash seat was a crevice that looked as if there was a missing carving.

"Here the missing turquoise green candle will sit. This will protect the Coracle from ever getting into the wrong hands ever again. It should be in the chest. Once the candle and holder is secured on this seat, they should then both unite, send a glow to the Hugglett spoon which will provide us with the future strengths and powers we've lacked lately," explained Ivor.

"Let's hope it's in the chest then. What we've gone through and all the family we've lost Ivor, was it worth it?" asked Gari as he cradled the casket of dead cats once more and walked away.

"Let's move the treasure into the castle Ivor. Gari's still upset," said Geraintus trying to smooth a tricky situation that was arising.

"I'm to blame Geraintus, I should have been more forthcoming about family business and the Croggs," explained Ivor. Before he could elaborate, the commotion from outside made Geraintus rush out in a hurry to help.

Wibbly and Millie barged through the small gate with the treasure chest in the middle of them. They continued straight into the castle, not stopping as the chest was very heavy and they had Hopkin and the Eagles right behind them.

"Ivor get ready to help with Molly. I'll bring the coracle in after you."

Hopkin came round the corner with the stretcher flown by the Eagles above, a beak carrying each pole. Hopkin had his hand on Molly's head, murmuring soothing spells as they moved.

"Quick, we need to get her inside."

Ivor paled significantly when he saw the state of Molly and briskly waved his hand as Hopkin and the Eagles continued into the Castle, where Gari had prepared a recovery room. Even he hadn't been prepared for the sight that confronted him as he started muttering soothing spells also as Hopkin and Ivor moved her on to the bed.

The Eagles shuffled outside, and knew they had to wait before they could be transformed to their original Knight status.

"Get the emergency magic lotions from the larder Ivor we need to knit her whole body back to life," instructed Gari as he started to examine her.

"Is she alive?"

"Barely."

Gari ushered Hopkin out of the room as Ivor came in with various contraptions. They closed the door and Hopkin didn't argue.

Geraintus fetched the coracle and Hugglett spoon, bought the cats casket inside and secured the castle. He placed the treasures alongside the Golden Treasure chest and prayed they would start communicating with each other and more importantly send Molly a mystical aura to help her recover.

Wibbly, Millie sat outside the room waiting for the dwarf and wizard to restore her and bring her back to life.

The Eagles stood outside waiting to be transformed to warriors and became very agitated again when told that Molly had the codes and no one else. What if she didn't make it?

***

Hopkin found the turquoise green candle in the chest and placed it on the coracle. The treasures all glowed and sent a wave of power through the wizard as Hopkin smiled. They would all gain their strength within days. He was pleased. The turquoise stone already in Molly's collar would help save her.

He went to a quiet corner in the castle to read the brown files and parchments he'd discovered earlier. The codes to spell the Eagles to Warriors were inside. He needed to read every single parchment and to find the ultimate proof that this treasure had always been theirs. Hopkin was still reading documents as Ivor came out of the sick room to find Geraintus.

"We need flowers, borage and as many ants as you can locate, can you all find some quickly. Wibbly, we need toads and snails at once."

Wibbly and Millie disappeared as instructed and Geraintus went to the whispering fig tree, where the borage and wildflowers grew. There was no sign of any messages from the tree but a wave of recognition that Molly was sick. Geraintus took an armful of flowers back to the kitchen as Wibbly and Millie bought in creepy crawlies, ants, toads, and everything disgusting on Ivor's list. Gari was soon out of the sick room to make a poultice of the creatures and ants.

Wibbly and Millie helped, they all had a bowl each of the ant mixture as they covered Molly from head to tail with the poultice. This was intended to knit her wounds and body together.

"The ants should start to work quickly," said Gari as Ivor started to mumble spells and chants.

Molly in a coma

Geraintus walked in with a nod from Hopkin in the corner, the Eagles were beginning to get agitated. They wanted their identity returned, after what they'd done for their master. Geraintus had informed them that Ifor AP Meurig had been killed in the battles with Owain, but the Eagles were no longer being patient.

"Ivor can you help them, I know you've got Molly to deal with but they're getting impatient, and I don't blame them."

"I thought it was only Molly who could transform them," said Gari as he continued to work on the dog.

"Gari continue here. Wibbly and Millie can help you. I'll see to the warriors right away," said Ivor swishing his triple cuffed sleeves as he waved for his shepherds' stick which followed him as they left the room.

Gari was even more annoyed with him at that moment but declined to say anything about how he felt, it could wait. He needed to save Molly and bury the cats and then he'd have a think about things, in his own time.

Ivor came outside with Geraintus, his shepherds' stick as lively as Ivor felt. The candle that was entwined around his stick was glowing and the thimble on the tip of the crooked end was a bright orange.

Hopkin stood in the hallway flustered and looked flushed which matched his pink robes.

"Whatever's the matter Hopkin?" asked Ivor feeling strong and powerful for the first time in a long time.

*"I'm going to the town hall tomorrow to register the treasure as ours and inform the publisher of the "**Welsh Wizard Weekly,**" to formally announce and confirm that we're the rightful owner of the treasure Ivor. I have the papers right here. There's also a few papers we need to discuss Ivor with urgency, this can't wait,"* whispered Hopkin as he became flushed in the cheeks."

"I'm going to transform the Eagles, Hopkin. We can discuss the papers when I come back," said Ivor knowing that he no longer could hide his secrets from the family. He'd forgotten what could be in the chest, but he knew he had to face it, regardless.

***

Ivor had known all along how to transform the trusted Eagles back to Warriors as Hopkin didn't waste any time. He spoke to Gari and Geraintus and knew that Molly was going to sleep for a long time. Geraintus decided to make his way to see Bedivere and Ivor would be able to bury the cats under the fig tree.

Hopkin prepared his repaired pink coach. He needed to register the treasures without delay. He hoped that no one would ever find out the secret in the treasure chest. He should bury it in the garden of Harlech or even Caernarvon castle for someone else to worry about in another hundred years.

Or he should spell it to disintegrate. Ivor needed to see the papers, but some of this cited Ivor. Ivor certainly needed to explain himself. He'd wait to have a chat with him and then he would depart for the Town

Hall, to register the treasure. He had a dilemma on his hands.

This family had lost enough members, but he wasn't the bearer of devastating news. Some of these documents would break the very foundation the Ap Llewellyn family stood for. No, he would bury or burn it and forget all about what he'd found once he'd spoken to Ivor and wait for an explanation. Then he would leave.

He would take his horse instead, which meant he had the perfect excuse to leave a bit sooner.

***

Blodwen Crogg in St. Clears was grief stricken but angry that her husband, Kentav Crogg, had been totally consumed with the so-called treasures that he'd got himself blown up in the process. She was terribly upset with him and in her state of distress had contacted Trent Crogg and asked him to help her.

Blodwen had sat for a few days and had reflected on her own demons, which at least she was grateful that Kentav had not known any of them. She was sure, he'd have mentioned the indiscretions in his papers, if he'd known of her illicit and tempestuous behaviour during the preliminary stages of their marriage. She had seven daughters; however, she had two other daughters who were born to two different suitors; neither of them her then husband Kentav Crogg.

She had kept this immense secret from everyone, including her two eldest daughters. Both had married and had their own children, to prestigious Knights. It would certainly get a bit messy if any of them found out. Silence was the best policy, she had decided.

The men involved knew of their daughters and both had agreed to keep their sordid secret to themselves. Their own reputation would falter if word got out that they had sired a child to a woman already betrothed to someone else.

Her first love had also been banished as she had been fifteen and with child. Her parents had re-located to save a scandal and had given her daughter away. This had been before her marriage to Kentav.

The second affair, she had sired twins, again she hadn't married Kentav at this point. She had become reckless when her first born had been given away. Her twins were also fostered, her parents becoming even more furious with her behaviour.

Her third affair had been during her initial marriage to Kentav.

Whilst this affair had been going on, Kentav Crogg had been consumed in building his carpentry business, and his ice cream factory business. He had spent an immense amount of time working on incredible techniques. He had assisted Ali in building those awful systematic creatures. She had been bored, and her dalliances had been innocent at the time.

She had stopped seeing both Wizards after falling pregnant by them both, literally eighteen months apart. Kentav had been no wiser. Thankfully, all her daughters looked the same, taking her looks and not Kentav's orange hair and freckles. She had been forced to give the twins away, and as far as Kentav was concerned he had fathered all their daughters. She had married Kentav as soon as the twins had been dispatched.

She couldn't explain to Trent Crogg that her illegitimate first born was entitled to the Llewellyn treasure as that would expose her secret, however she had sent enough information from Kentavs' papers to convince Trent, she had a claim.

***

In Manorbier, Trent was not happy being a husband to Katrin, a member of the Llewellyn family. He had agreed to return from Manorbier castle to find out what his sister- in- law had wanted of him. He felt a strange loyalty to her. He read some of the contents of the envelope that Blodwen had sent, to lure him to St. Clears as he smiled.

The fight for this treasure wasn't over; this was indeed the proof he needed. He would regain the treasures in honour of his brother's memory. He would prove to all in St. Clears that he wasn't the weakest brother by being the third born. Oh no, this was an opportunity for Trent to show that he was a Crogg of substance and that he had the leadership skills to put matters right, finally.

***

Chapter 15

Ivor's demons

Ivor returned to the parlour pleased with himself as he propped his shepherds' stick next to the treasure chest. He knew Hopkin was waiting to have a chat with him, and he couldn't put it off any longer.

"I'll sit with her Gari. Take some rest yourself, we'll get together in a bit," said Ivor as he could see that Gari was fraught and terribly distraught still.

Gari not happy with Ivor at all, managed to nod in agreement and left the room. Molly was showing signs of being stable, but it was going to be a long road to recovery.

Hopkin came in and Ivor baulked as he knew he had to answer subjective questions from the look on his face. He carried quite a few battered looking files as he composed himself and waved his arm in the air.

A cosy armchair appeared and placed itself next to Ivor and next to the bed, where Molly was hardly breathing.

"How is she?"

"Hopkin, she'll make it, but it's going to be a while before she comes round, the next few days are crucial. Thank goodness she's got nine lives," smiled Ivor who

tried to make light of a catastrophic end to their treasure hunting.

"It's not over yet Ivor. I shall take the legal paperwork to the town hall tomorrow morning but there's several birth certificates, a death certificate, and regal looking chattels in the treasure chest which I would like you to look at."

"Really?"

"Yes Ivor. I really would like you to be honest with me, we need some answers, before I leave. This could impact the register of the treasures. Let's start with this first file. Can you look at this certificate and tell me more. It's got your name on it."

Ivor paled and took the file from Hopkin. He opened it and paled even further and tried to compose himself. Before he'd disclose, he needed to know what else were in the files that could be incriminating about him. He read and re-read the certificate and cleared his throat.

"What else do you need to know?" he asked Hopkin.

"Apart from the Croggs explanation regarding treasures, which we'll deal with once I register the treasure, but there's this."

Hopkin handed a further file to him and got up towards the chest. As Ivor read the several pages of documents, Hopkin rummaged through the trunk and took out the two regal looking purses, he'd spotted earlier. He continued to look through to see if there was anything that looked suspicious, but there didn't seem to be anything else that looked urgent.

"These birth certificates are for my two children born to my wife at the time and they were officially adopted within a week," replied Ivor speaking quietly. *"Udemonora died in childbirth, Hopkin. I thought you knew, that's the death certificate, the dates are the same."*

"Yes, I remember she died suddenly Ivor, but I had no idea she had died in this manner. Why didn't you tell me you had a son and a daughter?"

"I had to give them away; I've tried to erase them from my mind. I'm not allowed to find them. However, if they are told of their status, they can find me. It's too painful to discuss Hopkin. They were both given names, but I have presumed and guessed the adoptive parents would have changed them, to make it harder for me to trace them."

"Is this why you're sometimes distant Ivor, Molly needs to know. Or is there anything else that you're not telling me and the family."

Ivor pondered for a few seconds, as he decided whether he should completely come clean but didn't have the guts to tell the great Hopkin. What would he think of him?

"No Hopkin, I'm distracted as I'm losing powers. My two children were handed to two separate very wealthy families and doing very well without this knowledge. I want to keep it this way. No-one needs to know Hopkin. The official status of these two kids are in my papers

which will be disclosed on my deathbed. I don't want to expose this now. What is in the papers that the Croggs are disputing?" asked Ivor holding his breath. Did he have to tell Hopkin?"

"I understand Ivor," said Hopkin feeling a bit of empathy for his friend. *"The Crogg statement is nothing really Ivor, forget that for now. But do you know what these are then and to whom do they belong. I've not seen these before,"* as he gave Ivor the two regal looking purses which made Ivor feel a bit faint suddenly, he was thankful he was sitting down, right at that moment.

"Goodness how did these get inside our treasure chest Hopkin?" queried Ivor aghast at this revelation.

"No idea Ivor, but we need to deal with them immediately as I don't want any repercussions once I've declared this treasure as ours tomorrow."

"Have you opened them, Hopkin?"

"No, I thought it best we did it together."

"Okay, open the bigger one first then," said Ivor holding his breath.

Hopkin took the first purse which was covered in white and brown horse skin and had a very heavy ornate clasp which had eroded slightly as Hopkin took a bit of time to prise the clasp open.

It eventually opened as Hopkin stuck his hand inside to get the contents out.

Ivor was beginning to feel funny as he had some inclination to whom this belonged. He continued and observed Hopkin who had now moved to the side table in the bedroom to disclose the contents fully. He joined Hopkin as he didn't really have much choice.

"*Goodness,*" exclaimed Ivor as he picked up various trinket looking stones.

"*This is a high neck brooch for a high-ranking lady of society and wealth Ivor. What are these items doing in our treasure chest?*" asked Hopkin a bit perturbed. "*This is another brooch too, it's got some engraving behind it, but I can't see it clearly. There's a few precious necklaces; these obviously are owned by someone important Ivor.*"

"*There's some parchment here Hopkin,*" said Ivor as he carefully opened the folded parchment and hoped there was nothing incriminating on it, regarding his misdemeanours.

"*Does it say anything Ivor?*" asked Hopkin who needed to clear this find up. He didn't want to have anything damning on his conscience or Ivor's for that matter.

"*It's very faded, we need to get our parchment dust out with our back to front mirror, we should be able to read it that way,*" said Ivor dreading this part but he had no choice but to get it done. These purses clearly didn't belong to the Llewellyn family, and they'd had enough of treasure hunting already.

"*I'll get Gari,*" said Hopkin.

"*Can you keep the certificates from everyone Hopkin. That's my business and I don't want to disclose* this right now. I will tell everyone eventually. Gari isn't happy with me as it stands, this may make him feel even more contempt for me," asked Ivor.

"Yes, of course I understand. But you ought to tell Garibaldi, Ivor. He's devoted to you; he should be told."

"I will tell him eventually, once Molly's well, I promise Hopkin. He might know already as I employed him the same time it happened. Gossip then, he might have heard," said Ivor.

"Regardless Ivor, you need to have a talk with him and sooner rather than later. He needs to know all your demons and all the ones you're not telling me right now. I'm not stupid and neither are the family around you," retorted Hopkin as he left the room to fetch Garibaldi to help them find the owner of the purses.

Ivor sat in silence as he could hear Molly's irregular breathing. At least she was breathing. What a mess he'd made of things. He should just come clean right away and get it over with. He desperately wanted to open the second purse but thought against it, he was frantic to know if there was something else that could incriminate him in the other purse.

He racked his brains as he thought of the name of the owner of these jewels as his thoughts got interrupted as Gari and Hopkin returned.

"*What is it Ivor?*" asked Garibaldi as he came inside the bedroom with Hopkin. He carried the back to front mirror and a contraption to help them decipher the words on the faded parchment.

"We've found these chattels in the treasure chest. We ought to find the owners and get this sorted before Hopkin goes in the morning to register our treasure Gari. We don't need anyone objecting to our announcement," confirmed Ivor who sounded braver than he felt at that moment.

Chapter 16

More complications

Garibaldi guessed Ivor had a few more demons in his cupboard to the ones he already knew about. He decided to leave his master to tell him in his own time. He didn't need more headaches right now. Grieving over the cats was taking its toll. The findings of these chattels were more important to deal with than Ivor's past, unless they were connected.

"I think we need to go into the parlour with both purses and get Millie or Wibbly to watch Molly," suggested Garibaldi. *"She needs quiet."*

"Yes, that would be more appropriate," agreed Hopkin as he collected the two purses, swept the files under his arm and they all left the bedroom to leave Molly in peace.

Millie crept inside the bedroom; she would be on first watch.

The treasures hummed as they walked into the parlour which was reassuring.

Garibaldi moved the mystical back to front mirror over the spare table and took the folded parchment from Hopkin as Ivor stood expectantly. He was beginning to feel quite faint.

He placed the parchment on the glass and whispered a murmured message to the mirror. He then placed some carbon dust from his special pewter box and swept it over the document carefully using his delicate brush made from peacock feathers and the odd hen. They waited after Garibaldi had completed the task as he continued to murmur some spell, which neither Ivor nor Hopkin could decipher.

The Hugglett spoon was wriggling out of its purple pouch and the golden coracle twitched as if annoyed. The wizards and Gari ignored the treasure and concentrated their minds on the parchment. They knew patience would prevail.

"Look its changing form," whispered Ivor dreading this really.

"Shhh Ivor, give it a few more minutes," whispered Hopkin who sensed Ivor was in a bit of a panic.

The parchment twitched and spluttered again as if it were about to wake up suddenly. The carbon dust moved around the document as if writing the note again. It was a few minutes before the document was transcribed on to the backward mirror as Ivor held his breath. Gari had a notebook in readiness for when Hopkin read the message albeit it was backwards.

"Ready Gari, here it is," said Hopkin who read it through before reciting it aloud.

"Inheritance to be claimed on marriage of first born. Claude Perrault of Versailles.

Ivor balked at this as who's first born.

"Do we know any of the Knights from Versailles Gari?" asked Hopkin who could see Ivor was a mess for some reason.

Gari noticed this too and shrugged, he had no idea at that moment.

"Why don't we open the second purse to see if there's anything similar in that one. This doesn't belong to us either, we might as well deal with all this right away whilst Molly's recovering. This has nothing to do with her," said Gari hinting at Ivor to say something.

"Yes, you're right, we need to sort this out while she's recovering," said Ivor relieved so far nothing incriminating had become known.

Hopkin started to prise the same antique clasp of the second purse as this was as rusty as the first one. It obviously hadn't been opened for a long time either. It eventually creaked open as Hopkin turned it upside down to the side of the backward mirror.

Several artefacts appeared including a lock of hair. A gold coin pendant which was embossed with a ruby stone and studded with turquoise stones. There was a gilded horse harness mount as an accessory. A ruby feathered hair accessory for a lady of wealth and another parchment. The lock of hair was entwined in the hair brooch. The hair was black.

"Is there a lock of hair in the other purse Ivor?" asked Hopkin as he studied the treasures.

"I'm not sure," as he examinaed the brooches. *"Oh goodness look, the back of the high neck brooch is open, it's got a lock of hair inside, yes, but its fair,"* baulked Ivor feeling a bit faint again.

"Okay we have a lock of fair and black hair, that's a start," said Garibaldi. *"What does the parchment say Hopkin?*

"It's just as faded, I think written the same time as the other one, I can't read it. You'll need to do the same magic on this one Gari. Let me place it on the mirror."

Hopkin had read it; he couldn't make out what it meant. He was too preoccupied, his mind was racing going through all the Knights he knew in France, he couldn't concentrate. He had no idea at that moment the relevance of the notes.

Garibaldi addressed the parchment in the same manner as the first one as it twitched in recognition of being seen. They watched in silence as the parchment made a few turns and suddenly it sighed and stopped moving. The transcript was sent to the backward mirror as Hopkin read the note aloud.

"Evanora, first born of age, male to thy body. Charles Perrault."

Goodness it's the same knight or two brothers, we need to find out?" asked Ivor relieved there was nothing to incriminate him.

"We need to get our encyclopaedias out and all our reference books right away. We need to return these

to the Knights, or Knight as they shouldn't be in our possession," declared Hopkin.

"*I couldn't agree more,*" said Ivor. "*I would like us to sort this out immediately and get the treasures back to the rightful owner before Molly wakes up. It will give us something constructive to action. I still think Hopkin you need to register our own treasure at once tomorrow, we mustn't waste time announcing we're the First Family of Wales,*" said Ivor.

"*Ivor's right Hopkin, we must declare the treasure as found and ours immediately,*" said Garibaldi intrigued with this new finding. He needed to get the books out right away to start looking for the owners of the purses.

It was going to be a long night as Gari, Hopkin and Ivor left the chattels in the parlour, locked the door, and decided to set up at the dining room table to find the answers.

Wibbly and Millie had been informed as they supervised Molly as the wizards and Gari started to look for information about Knights in Versailles or in that region that they might know.

"*Shall we ask Geraintus and Bedivere to come over to help us?*" asked Ivor.

"*Let's see if we can decipher this quickly tonight, if not, we'll call them at first light,*" said Garibaldi his fingers crossed they could sort this without major problems.

"*The encyclopaedia of Knights,*" was open at the table as Ivor started to scour the information. Hopkin, who wasn't at his best on written theories, started to look for the artefacts they'd found. His **"*Artefacts of wealth,*"** book that Hopkin had borrowed from a prestigious wizard last month was becoming extremely useful. He was glad that as, yet he hadn't returned it. He was grateful suddenly that he hadn't. He poured through the pages and prayed they'd find the information about the two brooches and the other artefacts which would help them to locate the actual owners.

The locks of hair bothered him the most, this was more than artefacts, this had something to do with indiscretions, he put that thought aside for the moment. And who was Evanora?

Chapter 17

Versailles

Charles Ferdinand Artois sat at his ornate oak panelled desk at his ostentatious home in the heart of Versailles. He was a happy rotund man and in front of him were many papers. These papers were in files adorned with different coloured ribbons and they were being read in the order they were given to him this particular morning.

There was nothing significant in these papers to his knowledge. They were mostly government business and information with relation to his estate, which was vast.

He watched his daughter and granddaughter play on the lawn outside. Olwenna was trying to teach her fifteen-year-old daughter, how to play boules. He smiled as he watched them. They were both fair skinned and both sported long fair hair plaited with ribbons. They were laughing as Olwenna gave Leonora more instructions. He was thankful his wife was fair otherwise he was sure some of his closest aides would have made pertinent comment regarding their birth right. People were so nosey these days.

He was also glad that the adoption had gone smoothly and that there had been no communication whatsoever from the Wizard, who he knew was still alive and a prestigious noble person in his community. He had fulfilled his commitment of no contact, but it was time to inform his daughter. The agreement had stated that on her thirtieth birthday he would tell her, that she was adopted. He was dreading this conversation as was his wife, but a promise was a promise. He had a week to get his head round it.

The papers that were stacked in front of him all looked a bit worn. Some worse than others. He picked up the two files with purple ribbons, these looked worse than the others.

He read the files with interest and more concern than anything. There were interesting statements in the file. He placed the file back on the table and opened the second one.

His demeanour changed when he read the second file. The contents covered all of Ivor Ap Llewellyn's treasure hunts and his reputation of being the First Wizard family to retain the title of First Family of Wales, even though there was an impending treasure not yet claimed.

Why was the file important to him, wasn't the issue. The copies of the birth certificates were significant, his adopted daughter was a twin. He pressed the gong by the fireplace as his trusted butler scurried in.

"Sir."

"Can you inform my wife I'd like to see her once she returns from her bridge tournament, Ivan."

"Certainly sir."

Olwenna had married Phillipe Delacroix, who was a descendant of Louis XIIV, and he was the direct heir to the Versailles fortune. Along with the Artois fortune, Olwenna and indeed her daughter would be extremely comfortable for the rest of their days.

He had no idea the implications that might arise as Olwenna had a brother. He was sure that wouldn't matter, but to be sure he needed to have a chat with his adored wife of fifty-five years, she was always good in her rationale of matters that had arisen over the years.

There was no covenant in any of the papers and no instructions regarding the adoption apart from confirmation that Olwenna had to be told by her thirtieth birthday. Once she turned thirty, her biological father had the right to trace her and declare her as his own. They hadn't changed her birth name as they had liked it, thus Charles knew this would therefore make it easier for her natural father to track her down, if he indeed wanted to.

Charles was sure that the Great Wizard Ivor Ap Llewellyn would indeed want to meet her. He didn't have a problem with the inevitable, but he had a problem bringing up the subject of her birth right as Olwenna was so happy, he didn't want to spoil what she had. He also didn't want it to spoil his relationship with her either, but that was him being a bit selfish. He sighed.

What will Olwenna's reaction be, he had no idea. He knew she was a remarkable sensible and level-headed woman, and he was sure he was making a mountain out of a mole hill. Knowing she had a brother, might pique her interest, but he was equally curious where the brother was, and if indeed he knew he had a sister.

Phillip Delacroix was currently in battle with a few of his trusted allies. The knights with him currently included the Perrault brothers, Jacques de Molay and Bertrand de Guesclin. They were in the process of securing Navarre and the town of Rennes in the North. They had been fighting for a few months and were not due to return until the towns had been made safe.

They had formed an alliance with the English to ensure these towns remained in their ownership, even though they were on French soil.

The men had joined forces when they had spent six months in York, well over a decade earlier. They had become staunch friends even though the Perrault brothers had joined them much later in the day. The two knights had married by the time the Perrault brothers had arrived, however through a commitment to the current King, the knights had continued to battle, leaving their estranged wives back in Wales waiting for them.

Prior to their wives leaving the York estate, two ladies had arrived a year earlier to support the war effort and to support the wounded. The two girls had needed to leave home as their mother had more than a few children to look after. As they were both older than the other children, the two girls had volunteered to help at York House for a year.

To their parents delight they had both found a Knight each to marry and had become settled at York House until the Perrault brothers arrived. Charles and Claude Perrault were very charismatic, and it wasn't long before both ladies were having an affair with one of the brothers and unbeknown to each other.

They had left for St. Clears, both expecting babies and they both knew that the two babies didn't belong to their respective husbands. Both confessed to each other on their way home in a silver encrusted carriage, befitting two ladies married to two well regarded Knights.

They both made a pact immediately that this knowledge was not going to be shared anywhere and they both agreed that the disclosure of their actual imminent babies' father, must never be known. It would complicate everything, and the girls also agreed that there should be no more dalliances. They giggled all the way home but also knew how serious this was if their husbands ever found out. Especially if they found out, who had sired their first born.

The only worrying factor was that their husbands had befriended the two brothers, but the ladies were sure that the brothers would never confess their sins. The Knights would behead them, no question of that.

Fifteen years later, and all was well. The two ladies had borne two sons and there was harmony in both marriages. The Perrault brothers had kept their word and had not made a claim on the children. Neither lady had born any other children either and the two boys were doted on by their respective dads.

There had been no significant dramas over the years and the two women had supported their mother through losing their Dad, but suddenly significant changes started to take affect which would create uncomfortable issues for the two older daughters.

They were both aware of their dad's obsession with the Llewellyn family and were tired of hearing his insistence that he was owed. They had no idea what he meant and neither had Blodwen. Blodwen had shown the two girls their Dads' paperwork which did put a different slant on the obsession Kentav had had with the Llewellyn treasure.

They had both retired home to their respective houses in the Amman Valley, West Wales and didn't think no more of it. It had nothing to do with them, they didn't want to get involved at all.

Chapter 18

The family make a discovery

"*We need some more help Ivor,*" said Garibaldi not really understanding why Ivor was in a hurry to find the owners of the purses. Couldn't it wait until Molly was fixed as her mystical persona could help them.

"*This isn't Molly's problem, it's ours,*" said Hopkin as he realised something he'd read in the artefacts book.

"*What have you found?*" asked Gari.

"*Look this high neck brooch belongs to the Perrault estate from the Loire valley of France. The Perrault brothers own jointly the Chateau de Miniere and the chateau De"Issay. Both have extensive acreage and are thriving exporters of fine wines and health products which are organically home grown on the estates. According to this, they are extremely wealthy, and we need to look up the aristocratic encyclopaedia. We need to know all about these brothers and quickly,*" said Hopkin as a large frown showed on his brow. "*We need to know who they're related to and what's the connection to us. Ivor, if you have anything to say, I suggest you tell us now. We need to contact them, the sooner the better.*"

"I can tell you both right now, I've never heard of the Perrault brothers, believe me," said Ivor equally flummoxed.

Hopkin and Gari could see that Ivor was actually telling the truth. Ivor went in search of the Aristocratic encyclopaedia ; he was relieved but truly had no idea why these purses had arrived in this chest.

"Have you found any information on the other chattels yet Hopkin?" asked Gari as he was trying to negotiate a massive bible sized book to the table. It had detailed maps of Europe and all the battle destinations past and present. *"I thought we best look up where the current fights are occurring."*

"Good thinking Gari," said Hopkin as he was scouring the encyclopaedia for the other chattels they had found.

Ivor returned with yet another massive encyclopaedia which was titled, **"the Knights of Europe."** *"I just thought it a clever idea to get Bedivere over, he's good at finding royalty and Knights. He'll be useful right now. I've sent a message for him to get here as soon as he can."*

"Yes, the more eyes the better," said Hopkin as he turned a page and gasped aloud.

"What is it?" asked Ivor and went to look at the page as Gari also stopped what he was doing.

"Oh my, the gold coin pendant. It's the same as the one we've got. What does it say Hopkin?"

"The gold coin pendants were handed to victorious knights after a successful battle. It is a tradition to give the pendant to a loved one or a person who was betrothed or a close family member. All the gold pendants issued have a serial number and an image, which reflect the precise location of the battle, and the serial number is traceable through the vaults of the town hall, where the actual knight to which it was presented."

"Once Bedivere gets here, I'll get him on to the serial number," said Gari. *"Keep looking for the other brooch, Hopkin."*

As Gari mentioned the word Bedivere the front door opened suddenly as if a gust of wind had propelled it open. Wibbly couldn't stop it. Bedivere had sent Elijas' trunk over and it slithered over the parquet floor, missing the dining room table with all the books and paperwork by inches.

***

Blodwen was pacing the carpet in the front room; she couldn't get to grip with the information Kentav had left her. She was also worried about her deep dark secrets of which there were more than one. The last thing she wanted was for her two eldest to find out the truth. Yes, she was meant to tell them at some point but to date she had been too embarrassed and too scared to tell either daughter who their true fathers were.

The trouble was they had different fathers; what would they think of her? The two men were alive, and she wondered if they were keeping an eye on them.

Both had promised to stay away, and to date both had fulfilled their obligations and her wishes. Oh, what a blinking mess!

To put more cats amongst the pigeons, she had another older adopted daughter. This was the reason her parents had moved location as she'd been expecting a baby out of wedlock and at the time, she had been underage. This child, and another daughter had been given away. Adopted much to her dismay and horror and to this day she had not informed her first suitor, her very first love of the consequences of their innocent love.

Furthermore, what would Kentavs' actual four daughters think? These four were Kentav's girls. They would lose all faith in her. How would they react to knowing they had three illegitimate sisters and a brother; one adopted but the two eldest right now had other fathers.

She swallowed hard, she felt faint. This was confusing even for her. She knew that one day all this would come back to haunt her. Her behaviour had been shocking, but she couldn't help herself. In a way she was glad Kentav wasn't here, he'd have blown a gasket and strangled her or at least she would have been banished from his and her daughter's lives. Especially if she had told him who the three suitors had been. He would have gone berserk. She would take this information to her grave but then she ought to tell them, it was only fair on the grandchildren.

Both daughters were not short of wealth with their current husbands, why rock the boat and cause upheaval. The girls deserved to know but until she felt it forced upon her; she was too much of a coward to tell them. Her adoptive daughter, she had no idea where she was, or her actual name although she had named her Elizabeth.

She placed all these misbehaviours to the back of her mind.

It was more important to see Trent and decide around Kentav's papers that the Llewellyn treasure needed to be contested.

***

"Found it," declared Hopkin.

Bedivere and Geraintus both walked in as Hopkin found the second brooch in the encyclopaedia, as Ivor and Gari joined him to see what the information said. Hopkin read it aloud.

"The ruby cast stoned hair brooch is unique to the owner and is handed to a betrothed lady on marriage or for the first born. The brooch is hand made with a loop to house a lock of hair. The signature on the clasp discloses the source of the purchaser, who by the law of the given land, must declare his or her identity on this rare purchase as only a hundred were ever crafted in this way."

Bedivere was in full swing as he listened to Hopkins statement as he examined the brooch in question.

Geraintus decided to get his note book out as he was useless in deciphering messages. He was better at note taking.

"Do I need to call on the Owl contingent, for messages?" asked Geraintus.

"Not yet Geraintus, let us examine the facts as we know it first," said Bedivere as he continued to examine the chattels. Both Bedivere and Geraintus knew it was best not to ask, where theses chattels had come from.

"Right, we have a fair lock of hair, a black lock of hair, two prestigious brooches both are handmade, and would have been commissioned, and a gold coin which was only presented to valiant knights in battle. There we have the clues so far and it looks as if the Perrault brothers are involved in some way, for whatever reason," summarised Hopkin mostly for Bediveres and Geraintus' benefit.

*"You don't mean Charles and Claude?"*asked Bedivere going quite pale.

"Yes, according to the parchments, they need to be found pronto," said Ivor intrigued his friend had baulked at the very mention of these two men. *"What do you know about them, Bedivere?"*

"They're not to be messed with, quite frankly. Whatever you've heard, they're yes very wealthy men but they're ruthless, which is why they have this reputation. They're remarkably successful men and Knights. We should be able to track them down quite quickly," said Bedivere. *"I'll send a message right away. We need to get hold of De Guesclin immediately. He spent time with*

them years ago. I know this because I had a servant at York House before he moved to Wales. He told me lots of stories about the goings on at that time."

"You don't mean Bertraud De Guesclin?" asked Ivor going very pale again.

"Yes," said Bedivere knowing this was a touchy subject for Ivor, but that wasn't his place to explain.

*"What has this Knight to do with the Perrault brothers. We think these artefacts belong to them. Why were they in our trunk? "*asked Gari frustrated as he could feel Ivor was again not forthcoming.

"Bertraud De Guesclin married my illegitimate daughter Imapianne, okay. Please don't ask me anything else," said Ivor as he stormed out of the room to his quarters in embarrassment. There was no way he was going to divulge the mother. He had no intention on disclosing that she was a twin either. That would be even more disastrous for his reputation. That information would go to his grave.

Silence ensued around the table as Gari tutted under his breath, as he hadn't expected that. He knew other things about his master. He obviously didn't know all the past. Bedivere and Geraintus had gone quiet as Hopkin decided to go outside for a bit of air. Things were indeed getting personal. No wonder Ivor didn't want Molly to be involved in this quest.

"Let's see if we can locate the Perrault brothers and this Knight, Bertaud," said Bedivere quietly as Geraintus

reached for the *"**the encyclopaedia of Knights book,**"* to start a search right away.

Geraintus had a few messengers outside waiting for errands, but as he and Bedivere had mentioned earlier, they were short of help.

The giant and wizard worked tirelessly as the others had disappeared for a while. Ivor needed to compose himself and face everyone. He was currently tucked up in his bed, after Gari had given him a strong sleeping draft. That was the only way for Ivor to tackle his own demons. Once rested Ivor may feel more positive to share more information.

Hopkin needed to get his head round that Ivor had more past skeletons than all the wizards he knew put together. The family had a problem, but he was scheduled to leave in the early morning to the town hall. At least he could get away for a day. Hopkin had no past skeletons, that he knew of. He was utterly ashamed of Ivor, but it was not his place to comment or criticize anyone, least of all Ivor himself.

He was no good in deciphering these issues. He would leave shortly as the sooner he registered their own treasure, the quicker he could return to assist in this awkward and complicated find that they'd discovered. He went outside for a bit of air and left Bedivere and Geraintus pouring over the large encyclopaedias on the table.

"I meant to ask you Bed, what's in the box you brought with you?" asked Geraintus needing a break from all this reading.

"Oh, I forgot, it belongs to Gari. I was handed it at Eddlee's Hornblov audience when I went to ask for help. I need to give it to Garibaldi, I'm sure it belongs to him, or the family at any rate."

As if on cue Garibaldi appeared from Ivor's chambers.

"What did you say Bedivere?" asked Gari hearing the last bit.

"I forgot when we arrived to hand this to you. Someone found it and asked at Eddlee's meeting if it belonged to someone as it kept twitching. I'm sure I've seen this with you. Can you check it's yours, Gari. I did promise to return it back to Eddlee if it's not," explained Bedivere who handed him a traditional hat box which he'd brought with his overnight sac."

"Oh, my goodness, it's my porkaht," exclaimed Gari as he held it to his chest. He checked it, as it seemed to twitch knowing it was with the right owner.

"What's the significance Gari?" asked Geraintus who didn't know much about the family past or background and was becoming more knowledgeable about the family's indiscretions than anything else right at that moment.

Garibaldi checked the pork pie hat over and nodded it was his masters, Ivor. He checked the red satin ribbon and saw that the secret lining had been exposed but the parchment and lock of hair was still intact.

He said nothing, again it wasn't his place, and this would add even more confusion and despair to the shared confessions, that the wizards had had to face over the past twenty-four hours. He thought quickly as he needed to answer Geraintus' question.

Hopkin came back from outside, having needed a quick fix of some substance to keep him going as he watched Gari inspecting the porkaht in detail.

"Oh, you've found it Gari, Ivor was only saying a few days ago in between our treasure hunting that he had mislaid it. Is it intact?" he asked as Gari realised Hopkin knew what secret lay inside it.

"Yes Hopkin, its intact. This belongs to Ivor; he was given this many moons ago and has a special place in his heart. At least we've found it. It needs to sit with the treasures. There is no significant detail around it Geraintus, it's just a special hat handed to Ivor, it's just a sentimental hat, that's all," said Garibaldi as Hopkin nodded in acknowledgment. Neither of them were going to elaborate and both of them realised that they may know another indiscretion, which neither was going to mention.

Ivor stood behind him, pink with his own knowledge of the hat and agreed. He'd divulged enough about his past already; they were not going to get part two out of him. He was more intrigued to know about the connection of the Perrault brothers to his treasure chest. He couldn't fathom what the connection was even though he'd had a good deep sleep.

"Who else has seen this close up?" asked Ivor taking it from Gari.

"Eddlee Hornblov," said Bedivere as Ivor visibly paled again and went to place the hat amongst the treasures and said nothing.

"I'll get a brew. We need to sort this out as Hopkin is about to leave for the town hall," said Gari who needed to change the subject right away.

"Before you do that Gari, everyone, I need to show you what I've discovered in Elijas' Trunk, which he has bequeathed to me of all wizards on his deathbed," said Bedivere knowing the unwelcome news for Ivor wasn't going to get any better.

"Let's have it," said Hopkin. Best to get all the messy nonsense of family secrets out in the open all at once. Gari was looking more like thunder by each passing moment, his disappointment evident in his face regarding his master.

Bedivere moved to the trunk which had parked itself by the fireplace as it had careered in on its own volition. He opened the trunk, and it showed a colourful burgundy lining of significant value.

"Goodness, this looks like a trunk from the royal household," said Gari intrigued but more worried than ever.

"Yes, that's what I thought," said Bedivere," *and it is from the Delacroix estate in Versailles of all places. This is what I've been researching while I waited for you all to settle in, before sharing the details with you."*

"Does this have a link to the Perrault brother's then?" asked Geraintus.

"That's the research we've been doing Geraintus, I didn't say anything as I wasn't ready to tell you all, but it seems like the secrets are finally being shared. I wanted to tell you that Elijas wasn't here as a family friend, he was in fact spying on the Llewellyn family."

Gari stormed out to make that tea, he'd had enough. *I'm going to get Ivor, he needs to hear this,"* he said.

Ivor returned from his quarters looking even more dishevelled as before and held his head up high and sat at the dining room table.

"What's this about Elijas," he asked.

"Well, our Elijas wasn't exactly a loyal friend, Ivor. We all blamed Tudor for being a traitor of sorts, but Elijas wasn't exactly our friend either," explained Bedivere.

"Can you get to the point," said Hopkin, *"I need to leave for the town hall and I'm going by horse not coach."*

Bedivere took an assorted pile of papers out of Elijas trunk, some had purple ribbons adorning them, which were the ones Bedivere placed on the table.

"These papers, and I've read them all twice, categorically shows that Elijas had orchestrated the second ambush at Symonds Yat, and he had been given

chattels to thank him for all the information he has been passing to Charles Perrault, which is why I'm even more furious than earlier, "said Bedivere looking straight at his friend Ivor.

"All right, all right, I still don't have a connection to Charles Perrault," said Ivor.

"You must have Ivor, Elijas has been passing him our spell formulae's, our castle information, and all sorts of Llewellyn matters, I gather from what I've read. Elijas was instrumental in hiding the two purses, of which he has placed them in that trunk many moons ago and eventually befriended me and us all," declared Bedivere.

"So, this Knight, these brother's then who you claim are ruthless and not to be messed with has pertinent information about me, or us the Llewellyn family which they will use at some point for their own financial gain," asked Ivor.

"Yes, but not financial I don't think it's anything to do with finances, he's a self-made man as is his brother, but there's something more important than wealth, Ivor."

"Heirs and status," said Hopkin as he walked out and slammed the front door, he'd heard enough.

"Whatever you all think of me right now," said Ivor, as Gari returned with a strong brew of Aloe Vera tea, *"I have no idea what these brothers want of me or our family. I haven't heard these names until now, or the Delacroix estate."*

"There is something linked to us, these purses are hidden in our treasure chest for a reason, Elijas had the answer, we will need to tread carefully, hand the chattels over and hope that whatever claim or whatever he wants eventually, he'll tell us, and we can deal with it," said Ivor.

"How much snooping around did Elijas do in your cave Ivor, over the time we knew him?" asked Garibaldi trying to get his head round more indiscretions of some kind. He couldn't keep up.

"He was never really alone here," said Ivor.

"Yes, he was on occasions, Ivor. Plenty of time for him to go through your bureau, which even I haven't even gone through," said Gari feeling a bit foolish on behalf of Ivor.

"Don't blame yourselves," said Bedivere, *"None of us knew, we at least have found out who attacked Tudor, they were obviously looking for the purses. Now, we can hand them over civilly,"* said Bedivere.

They all knew as they sat quiet for a moment that whatever the Knights wanted, it wasn't over. Someone would have to tell Molly once she'd come through this last trauma. It wasn't Molly's fight or dilemma; she'd done her part.

Chapter 19

The battlefield in Rennes.

Garibaldi returned to the dining room with another large pot of Aloe Vera tea and a slate plate piled high with Welsh cakes. He plonked them on the table as Bedivere and Geraintus were pouring over the encyclopaedias to find the Knights mentioned.

"Where's Hopkin," he asked.

"He's gone to Cardiff to register our treasure in the **"Welsh Wizard Weekly,"** *we can't leave it any longer,"* stated Bedivere.

"Yes, I agree," said Gari. *"Ivor can you help, we need more eyes going through these books."*

"Yes, that would be helpful," said Geraintus as they all agreed it was going to be an all-nighter.

"Send my friend a note, Geraintus. Write a pebble to Charles Artois. He's in Versailles, he may be able to shed a light where these guys are right now. That might be quicker than ploughing through these books," suggested Bedivere.

"Right, I'll sort it," said Geraintus as he got up to the living room. He reached to the mantlepiece where a sack of pebbles, in all assorted colours were parked for immediate pebble sending at short notice. *"Which colour shall I send?"*

"Send the feathered one, that requires urgent response, Charles will know that" replied Bedivere as he paused. He'd found something. He waited for Geraintus to send the message. *"Come here, look I've found something."*

Ivor suddenly appeared and he looked refreshed and ready for any questions. Gari followed him as they all sat round the table as Bedivere read out what he'd found.

"Bertraud De Guesclin is a French Knight, and he's in battle in Rennes as we speak. He has a chateau in Provence, and he has a base in West Wales. That's interesting," said Bedivere as Ivor squirmed but didn't venture any more information.

"Where in West Wales?" whispered Ivor. He wasn't aware she was this close. *"Amman Valley. To find him, we only need to go to the town hall. That's easy. Now we know where his base is, that makes life easier."*

"What's he got to do with the Perrault brothers, as the items we've found actually seemingly belongs to them and not this Bertrand fellow?" asked Gari.

"I know Bertrand and I have a feeling he knows the Perrault brothers. Charles in Versailles, my friend will know more. That's why I wanted to know where he's based. The Perrault brothers need tracking down. I would imagine if Bertrand were fighting in Rennes, the brothers are either there or not far away. Any joy Geraintus on the Knights encyclopaedia?" asked Bedivere.

Plop, plop.

"A feathered pebble Bedivere, are you expecting one?" asked Gari as he fetched it from Wibbly who was changing shifts with Millie.

"Yes, from Charles Artois in Versailles," confirmed Bedivere. *"What does he say?"*

Ivor held his breath as Garibaldi read out the message.

"Glad to be of service, Bedivere. My son in law is Phillipe Delacroix, feel free to contact him at the base in Rennes. He is with the Knights in question. Regards Charles."

"Look up Phillipe Delacroix," said Gari immediately as he could see in the corner of his eye that Ivor was becoming paler by the hour with this information. *"Anything you wish to add, Ivor?"*

"No, No, I've said all I need to say. I have no idea who this Phillipe Delacroix is Gari and why Elijas had his information in his trunk or what is the connection to me, us the Llewellyn family. Elijas was obviously sharing all our family goings on with them."

Geraintus and Bedivere could feel the tensions rising again and ignored it. Suddenly Bedivere turned the next page and said, *"Bingo."*

"Read it out," said Gari disappointed with Ivor.

"The battle for Rennes is being fought with King Edward who has been kindly supported by several Knights of the first order, namely Charles and Claude Perrault, Bertrand De Guesclin, and Jacques De Molay.

All these knights have formed a bond since their initial introductions at a mutual Knight's residence in York House, decades ago.

It was a pact of mutual friendship and personal agendas that these Knights decided to support the King in his quest to defend both Rennes and Navarre. There seems to be an unbroken and unsaid bond within the ranks of these men, which is unusual to say the least and remarkable since their friendships had been introduced none other than by their wives at the time."

"*Whatever does that mean apart from we know where they are,*" said Geraintus.

Wait, there's more," said Bedivere as he turned the page. "*The meeting prior to the men departing to Rennes had included the mercenary Jack Turk, who had no foundation for being there, however the Knights had departed as one. Jack Turk had an audience with all four men individually but none of the Knights would disclose the content of such dialogue to each other or to the onlookers, of which there seemed to be a gathering of interest outside the grand gates of the establishment."*

"*Oh my,*" said Ivor not hiding his shock at this statement read out by Bedivere.

"*What is it Ivor?*

"*Blodwen Crogg was Jack Turks' childhood sweetheart I believe. They went to a different schooling system to the average children. She moved away very suddenly and unexpectedly with her parents, which was* a long time ago. I haven't heard his name until now," explained Ivor.

"What's the connection to Jack Turk and her then and why are we involved. We still don't know why we have treasures that belong to the Perrault brothers in our possession," said Bedivere getting very frustrated with Ivor and the sooner Hopkin returned the better he would feel.

"Bertrand has married my illegitimate daughter, and it states that they were introduced to the Perrault brothers by the wives of the two knights. We need to find out the name of the wife of the second Knight and if there's a connection to us there. We know that my illegitimate daughter is one connection, but no one knows about this fact. I wouldn't think that Bertrand knows either. Don't forget, my biological daughter hasn't yet been informed that Charles Artois is in fact her adopted father. This has nothing to do with Bertrand de Guesclin, its two separate issues.

He did promise to inform me when he discloses to her. I've yet to receive that information, then we must assume Bertrand isn't aware of his wife's actual father. Bertrand met the Perrault brothers in York innocently but somehow there's a reason they've all become friends," summarised Ivor. *"I fulfilled the arrangement; I promised never to contact her. I have kept my part of the agreement, even though on occasions, when it's her birthday I do feel remorseful. To explain myself, my adopted daughter therefore will not know about my illegitimate daughter. I don't wish to discuss this anymore. I'm tired. My past isn't pretty, but I can promise you I have no idea why these artefacts are in our trunk and the connection to the Perrault brothers. I hope you believe me,"* said Ivor becoming weary of it all.

"Bedivere, this doesn't seem to be Ivor's fault, give him a break," said Geraintus as Ivor looked as perplexed as everyone else. Ivor walked out again; he couldn't deal with his own confessions.

"Obviously, Blodwen Crogg is in the thick of this I feel, but I have no other ideas. What do you all think?" asked Bedivere reaching out for a well-deserved chocolate biscuit. He sipped a strong Aloe Vera Tea that had something very potent in it, which he nodded at Gari, as indeed he needed it right now as did the others.

Millie and Wibbly came in to see them all as they reported on Molly's condition and confirmed the estate was quiet. They would continue to keep watch on the front gates along with Molly's well-being. They both could see there was a treasure hunt of a different kind being discussed and until they were needed, they would continue to keep an eye on Molly and look out for Hopkins return.

***

"Why did that idiot turn up and spoil things and how on earth has he found out?"

Charles Perrault and his brother Claude had nothing to be proud about but in their defence all they had wanted was a bit of fun. They had not told each other of their dalliances until much much later as the ladies of the two Knights had dearly departed to Wales, and both in the family way.

"*How did he know and what does he want actually?*" asked Claude.

"*I have no idea, he's looking for Elizabeth, I have no idea who she is, have never met an Elizabeth, especially a redhead, not really my type. Do you have any ideas?*"

"*None whatsoever, but he's more or less accused us of something we've done although he doesn't know we have done anything,*" said Charles a bit relieved. "*What did he ask Jacques and Bertrand, I wonder?*"

"*The same question maybe, do they know an Elizabeth.*"

"*Why interrogate us individually then, what was the sense in that. The poor man is obviously desperate to find her. Lizzie's in our circle but we haven't linked her to him. She's not a redhead, quite the opposite.*"

"*I have no Elizabeth on my radar.*"

"*Come on the others are waiting. Rennes can't be saved without us. We promised. Let's go.*"

"*What about asking Evanora she might have an answer?*

"*Don't get involved Charles, we've got enough on our plate.*"

***

Hopkin rode through the night with several new pieces of information swirling in his head. The most surprising piece of information was regarding Ivor. He had admitted to siring twins but during the investigation about the treasures they'd found out that he had confessed to an illegitimate daughter. He was not about to disclose the woman or witch he'd had the affair with. It was not difficult to work out as Ivor had had a bee in his bonnet about the Croggs for so long, it could only be Blodwen Crogg.

However, Hopkin knew something else, he was fed up with being on the back foot. That porkaht proved to him that there was another dark deep secret, that Ivor wasn't going to share. What else was he hiding? Gari knew about it, but he could see that Garibaldi didn't know everything either. What would Molly think?

He had no idea about the information in the porkaht, but he knew that the future of the Llewellyn empire was going to be seriously challenged at some point, and he needed to get ahead of it all.

However, he was assuming, as he had no proof. Whilst he was at the town hall, he would gather all the records about the Crogg children and all the birth certificates around each one, his curiosity was getting the better of him. He would also request all the birth certificates around Ivor Ap Llewellyn, he needed to know.

He turned round a few times as he cantered slowly through the streets towards Cardiff, knowing there were a few hours before the town hall opened its doors.

He had a friend in St. Fagan's, and he decided to pay a visit and rest a while until the morning.

Twice he turned round whilst he veered off course towards his destination. He was being followed; he could feel it. He hadn't spotted him or them, but he knew he was being watched. Whoever it was would have to wait. He would stay at his friends until mid-morning. There was plenty of time to register the treasure. It would draw out whoever was tailing him into the open. He reluctantly steered his trusted stallion towards the main building of the farm and a light went on in the main window.

They were expecting him. He would be protected here.

Chapter 20

More confusion

Hopkin opened the stable door of his friend's house at a sensible time of ten o'clock. His friend had confirmed who was tailing him and Hopkin could only smirk with victory. However, the victorious family couldn't yet celebrate until these treasures had been properly registered at the Town hall and inserted in the periodical. *"The Welsh Wizard Weekly, "* which was Owain's newspaper and all-important events by the law of the town halls, had to be declared in this paper as a matter of course.

Hopkin couldn't get the confession from Ivor from his mind. He not only was on a mission to complete the register of the treasures, but he was also going to request a copy of all birth certificates registered at the civic hall of Blodwen and Kentav Crogg and indeed Ivor Ap Llewellyn. If Ivor had more skeletons in his cupboard, then Hopkin wanted to know about them in advance of any more surprise treasures landing on the family doorstep.

The only sticking point about this request, he would have to hang around Cardiff for part of the day until the paperwork was compiled. Another issue which he had to ignore and justify later, the recipient's involved would receive a document to say that a request had been issued for said certificates and by whom.

As Hopkin was a very well-respected senior wizard in the community, he didn't feel this was a problem. He would deal with any objections. These objections would also be too late as by the time the papers were despatched Hopkin would have read the documents and saved them to his memory.

A risk worth taking if it meant he had the heads up of the past misdemeanours of the said parties. If indeed there were other skeletons to be unravelled. He hoped not, for Ivor's sake and the family in general.

He sent a pebble to Gari to explain he was temporarily delayed, and he would return by end of the day.

***

Bedivere and Geraintus had gone for a few hours' sleep as Gari was attempting to get Ivor to his quarters for some rest. It had been a long night and at three in the morning, it was decided to reconvene in the morning as Hopkin would also be on his way from Cardiff Town hall.

They had made several lists and Ivor's demeanour had become more defensive by the hour, which had ended the research for the time being.

Garibaldi was exhausted as he sat with Millie and Wibbly Alf and explained what had happened earlier. He was grateful they were there as he realised there was not enough help moving forward and he would have to have a chat with Hopkin about it on his return.

Molly was stable at last as Gari checked her again before Wibbly ushered him to his quarters, as Gari looked worse for wear himself. Millie would sit at the front door and keep watch as both dogs had the routine down to a fine art. The cats were still in the caskets by the open fire. Their burial had been placed on hold. These chattels they'd found had taken priority over a funeral service.

The whispering fig tree had no reports of any funny goings on and at three in the morning, there seemed to be a calmness about the place at last.

Millie wondered how long the calmness would last and shrugged. She was only glad she was here and nowhere else. She prayed Molly would wake up soon as she could help these wizards finish this new mystery much sooner.

***

Blodwen was feeling the pressure. This was the first time in over twenty years that her past misdemeanours had started to bother her. She knew it was time to tell her two eldest daughters, and she decided she had no choice but to speak to them individually and accept the consequences. Even though she had already sired a child before her sixteenth birthday, Kentav had not been aware that her two first daughters had also been illicit affairs. She knew that suddenly her impeccable reputation she had carved for herself with the help of Kentav was about to shatter.

She sent a communication pebble to both daughters and asked for their time for a personal chat. She prayed they would see her individually and not together. She continued to pace the mat in front of the hearth as she waited for their response.

While she would be explaining her disgrace, would that be the right time to inform them both that they had an elder sister that had been adopted. And would Imapianne go berserk once told she had a brother somewhere. Or was that going to be too much in one go. She sighed.

Plop, plop.

Ah that hadn't taken long, she sighed again as she picked it up from the mat, sat down on the couch and opened the very grand ribboned pebble.

This is a bit swank of the girls; she thought as she opened it. She read the message and went pale, then went crimson red in the face and she threw the message into the open fire as her hand shook with dread and fear. Someone had requested all birth certificate's citing her and worst of all, it was the well-respected Hopkin Paulinus, Ivor's confidante, and senior wizard.

Had he told Hopkin? What was Ivor's intentions? She knew after Imapianne had turned thirty, he was able to make connection of his free will. Her daughter had just turned thirty-two, what had happened suddenly for this to happen.

The worst part, Imapianne would also receive the same notice, which would raise her curiosity at least, as would Evanora. She took a long breath, if these girls were going to be informed, then Jack Turk would get a notice too. She had been forced by her parents to cite the accurate suitor on her adopted daughter's birth certificate. Lizzie would also be informed, wherever she was in the world. All of Hopkin's actions were now going to open a massive assortment of problems. Her own father had been adamant that the father of the child needed to know, even though he may never find out. It was only right.

She was feeling quite faint at these impending tricky meetings ahead. Why had Hopkin Paulinus had needed to request this information. Something was going on in the Llewellyn camp obviously and she was going to get dragged into it, whether she wanted to or not.

She ought to visit Ivor, however there were significant documents in the papers that Kentav had left which made her resist. This was personal about her. The treasures involved her marriage to Kentav; therefore, it was best to let Trent decide on how they should proceed.

She sat feeling numb and waited but dreaded for her daughter's pebbles to arrive.

***

The battle at Rennes was concluding finally. The Knights had been extraordinarily successful and had secured the town in its entirety and had also gained a few miles each side of the town. There they had commissioned soldiers to set up security positions for incoming and outgoing transport which would secure the township and the inhabitants from further potential take overs.

King Edward had been impressed and declared a success as they all followed the royal horse cavalry towards Navarre, who needed their support. Extremists and the King were occupying Navarre, and he took his extended Knights and entourage to the next town to gain control, that the French had temporarily lost.

It was an impressive site, and the Knights hadn't lost any team member or indeed there had been no casualties to date, and everyone were feeling exuberant and powerful as they should.

On approaching Navarre, the men set up camp and prepared a battle station to talk through the next takeover. A feathered bound pebble arrived at Phillipe Delacroix feet as he was attending to the horses. He read it with interest didn't understand the contents as he stuffed it into his breeches pocket. He would get that dealt with a bit later.

Once he re-joined the men, he handed the pebble message to Bertrand as he had no idea what it meant.

"I think this is for you," said Phillipe. *"My father-in law has sent it. Does it make sense to you?"*

"Let's have a look," said Bertrand, *"Bedivere AP Llewellyn requires an audience on your return. Please*

contact at once, a matter of personal treasure has been located which may belong to your estate. Charles Artois."

Claude Perrault went slightly crimson, but he was not facing Bertrand who didn't notice. How did Bedivere AP Llewellyn know about stuff?

"I know Bedivere quite well, I'll message him for you, Bertrand. I'll ask him exactly what's up as we're about to seize the town of Navarre," said Claude who needed to take control of this immediately. This could get out of hand and very awkward.

"That would be great, I don't know the family. I know their reputation of course, who doesn't but I have no idea why Charles would message me, instead of you either?" said Bertrand a bit confused.

"Leave the matter to me, I'll find out what treasure they're on about. Let's get on, we need to be in position right away," said Claude as he looked at Charles who was equally surprised.

They had both asked the respective women to send a lock of hair to them on the birth of their sons, which they had. The Perrault brothers had safely inserted this evidence in hand made brooches which had been safely deposited amongst other personal possessions. They had secured the purses to a treasure chest, years ago for safe keeping. Until this day they hadn't given this much thought.

"Did the girls register the births at all?" asked Charles quietly.

"We'll talk later Charles, I need to get in touch with Elijas," said Claude as he nodded in acknowledgment as they alighted their horses to get in position.

***

Ivor, Bedivere and Geraintus were suitably refreshed as they all sat round the table. They had decided they wanted an answer before Hopkin arrived, that was their challenge. They'd received a pebble to say he was slightly delayed, which gave them a bit more time to work out a plan.

Bedivere was waiting on a response from his last pebble to Phillipe Delacroix and he felt they would make swift progress once he knew their position.

Molly was breathing better, but still in a coma. Millie and Wibbly Alf were running the security with the aid of the whispering fig tree, and everything seemed calm, which was just as well.

Plop, plop.

Two pebbles arrived. One from Hopkin and one obviously from France as it had the Perrault brother's insignia on the front.

"Oh, lets open Hopkin's first," said Ivor who tried to stay calm.

"All treasures registered and will be announced this afternoon in the "Welsh Wizard Weekly." Delayed but on way. New treasures will need to be actioned sooner rather than later. H."

"Well, we know that" said Ivor a bit sarcastically.

Plop, plop.

"Another ribboned pebble, for you Ivor," said Wibbly as he dropped it at his feet.

"Oh, that's unusual," said Ivor.

"Do you want to open that before I open this one from France?" asked Bedivere.

"No open it," said Ivor as he began to get flustered.

"Request information on possessions that may be of value to my estate. Your humble servant. Charles Perrault."

Ivor had walked away to open his pebble and had squirmed with embarrassment on reading the message. It was confirmation that Hopkin Paulinus had requested all birth certificates in his name. He fainted and collapsed before he could reach for his walking stick to steady himself.

"Ivor!! Quick Geraintus, Bedivere, help me get him to his chambers."

Garibaldi stuffed the message into his trousers, he would read it later. The last thing he wanted was to embarrass his master further, whatever it was. Geraintus and Bedivere went back to the drawing room, both knew there was more to this find than they were being told.

Gari returned from the bedroom, and confirmed Ivor was asleep but in a state of shock for whatever reason. He wasn't going to elaborate on that last pebble, it wasn't his place.

"Send Charles Perrault all the information of the treasures we have and ask him when he can collect. We're happy to look after them if they are his. Also explain we don't have any explanation how they have appeared in one of our most protected treasure chests. The chest has been dormant for over several decades. If they can shed light on that, this would be appreciated. Something like that Bedivere, say, If these artefacts are yours including the locks of hair, we would be honoured to safe keep them until you are ready to collect. Sign it from Ivor Ap Llewellyn. Don't mention Elijas for now in case we're wrong."

"Yes done," said Bedivere as Wibbly took it and sent it off to goose who was always on call outside.

⸻◈⸻

Vaults at the town hall

Chapter 21

Hopkin Paulinus

Hopkin Paulinus had hovered around the town hall of Cardiff all morning. The treasures had been registered, at last and that had been seamless. He had requested for all birth certificates with Blodwen Crogg cited and the second request had been Ivor Ap Llewellyn. The elves had raised their eyebrows as he had written the second request but had said nothing.

They had shuffled down to the archives in the dungeons of the town hall, where all sensitive and personal documentation that belonged to all reputable wizards, head of established families, were kept in secured vaults. Permission had to be given for the average peasant to ask for such papers, but no one needed the great Hopkin Paulinus to explain his reasons for requiring such delicate information.

This was to protect powerful Knights,' Wizards and men in important positions to be caught out on their reckless infidelities, if they had any. Permissions for the average person, was indeed long winded and a laborious affair as the culprit if that were the right word, and by the local laws, had to be informed of such information being leaked from an official request. The information would also tell that person involved who had asked for the request but not why.

Hopkin sat in the vestry of the town hall patiently as he waited for the papers to be prepared and delivered to him by hand at the appointed hour. He fidgeted. He didn't really want to know what Blodwen had done in her life or Ivor for that matter but they both had crossed the line. The Llewellyn family were involved, these treasures had flagged up their innocent involvement.

He knew as well as Molly, when she came round from her coma, that there was enough demons in the Llewellyn camp. This extra involvement with outside foreign families was only going to make their immediate feud with the Crogg family more complicated.

He had realised who had been following him. Why the Wizard Mick had been tailing him, he had no idea. But was known to be the Eddlee Hornblov's lacky and unpaid sneak. Eddlee was the highest Wizard based in Cardiff. He had no issue with him. All very troubling but he shrugged. He di……

"Hopkin Paulinus, sir," shouted a tiny elf from the counters edge of the corner of the vestry. He was so tiny all Hopkin could see was his peak green cap which stood very tall.

"Yes here," he stated as he got up and his towering frame walked towards the tiny hand that held up quite a thick file to Hopkins' surprise.

"Please sign here sir," said the elf as he shuffled a document towards him on the counter. Hopkin could see the hat and his little hand but nothing else. He

smiled. He signed and the file was dropped on the counter.

"Thank you, that will be all."

He shoved it inside his grand cloak in his concealed pocket as the cloak flapped quite loudly as he strode very quickly out of the town hall and towards his horse.

He rode quickly to Penarth as he wanted to read the content before getting back to the Castle. He stopped at his favourite watering place and decided to pop in and have a glass of mead. Something told him, he would need it.

He sat in the corner; a few wizards acknowledged him as they recognised him. A few elves were in the corner playing cards. He waved for a tanker of ale as he disappeared and sat in the furthest corner of the tavern, which was a bit dingy in places. That suited him for this task.

He nearly choked on his ale as he read the contents of both Blodwen's past and Ivor's. The only troubling item with Ivor, there were three classified documents sealed until his will was read. He had no idea what they were and if they were birth certificates, they could be other documents pertinent to Ivor's estate. However, he had the three he knew of, the twins and one other. The elf had placed other files within this report, whether he should have or not, he didn't care at that moment. There was a file on Elijas MacQuaid, his sister Gabriella had an interest in the Llewellyn affairs. There was no suggestion of anything apart from that note. The note stated that one of the classified items were linked to her.

He knew this was none of his business and he would seal the read document's one he had finished with them. He knew that by now Ivor and Blodwen would have notices sent to them that he had read these very private papers.

He wasn't going to ask Ivor about Elijas's sister; it was best to save this information as knowledge was power. He would keep all this to himself, he would make his own investigations once all the unfinished business with the Crogg's were done and dusted.

Blodwen's business surprised him, who would have known. The findings were shocking and indeed quite repulsive. He was sure that Kentav Crogg had never known and for a moment he felt a bit of empathy for the Crogg. He was not going to discuss this revelation with anyone, however there was a huge issue, with the adopted girl of Blodwen's. He didn't know if he should warn Ivor or not.

It wasn't his business but Jack Turk a mercenary from Pembray, had involvements with Blodwen Crogg along with another prestigious wizard. He was totally dumbfounded. Blodwen had certainly had a colourful past. It was shocking. He would park this information until he felt he needed to share it. He would disclose if it meant harm to any of the Llewellyn's. It wasn't his business until it affected his family.

He left the tavern, got on his horse, and made his way swiftly towards Tongwynlais, Castell Coch where the wizards were waiting for him in earnest.

Forearmed and forewarned. That's how Hopkin wanted it to be.

***

A pebble had arrived at his feet very unexpectedly as he was conducting a family meeting. They were in the middle of a crisis and his sons were discussing their next request for mercenary support, but the pipeline of impending work was dire indeed.

"What are we going to do Dad?" asked Zack Turk.

"*Something will come up, have faith*," said Jack Turk as he opened the flamboyant ribboned pebble. He read the enclosed in silence, he baulked and went quite pale. He shoved it in his trouser pocket, not quite believing what he'd just read.

"*You okay Dad?*" asked Zack.

Yes, it will all be all right," said Jack not knowing what to make of the message and could he turn it to his advantage, he smirked.

⊷⊶◄❖►⊷⊶

Chapter 22

Beginning of the End

Hopkin rode quickly towards Tongwynlais and Castell Coch with information he wished he didn't have safely in his pocket.

There was quite a lot of outstanding issues to deal with, least of all these Knights. There was going to be a few terse conversations, of that, he was sure.

He wondered how much Garibaldi knew and he was impressed by his complete loyalty towards his master.

There was a few tricky moments to come, the mere fact that Eddlee Hornblov had read the inner lining of Ivor's porkaht, that was a bit disconcerting. He knew that that part of the past was classified. The fact that Ivor had been a playboy wizard had shocked him the most.

You never know people he thought as his horse cantered through the tall gates of Castell Coch to be greeted by Wibbly Alf.

It was only a matter of time before Molly came round from her coma. It was an idea to share everything with her and they could, as a family decide on this current predicament, or leave it alone. It was Ivor's problem, but the chattels found were worth an

Eddlee hornblov's tavern

immense amount but unless Ivor explained a bit more their hands were tied.

Their treasures had been found but past indiscretions could involve them in a completely new wave of treasure hunting. He sighed, it wasn't over yet, whatever it was. Family's always want what they think is theirs. Time would tell.

All he knew at that moment that this was maybe not the end of the treasure hunt, it was the beginning of something much more than that.

The Llewellyn Riddle

Death is imminent for a friend and not foe,

Use your magical, mystical power and mystical spell.

Eagles are coming; red kites or bats; no.

Find the clue, an ancient place with wishing well.

Purple is strong but there is turquoise blue.

Not to paddle, but to carry, Coracle Gold

Nesta, Helen of Wales, says it's true.

Treasure chest needs to be found and sold,

Magical, Mystical Molly, it's written in the mud,

You or your friends must not shed the first blood.

———◆———